THE DOVE

A NOVEL BY

CHRISTINE E. SCHULZE

To Aaron, my hero
To Eric, my hero for a time
To Sarah, Rachel, Hailey, Krystal, and Tiff, the infamous heroines
To Josh, Nathan, and Sam, the infamous heroes
To Amanda Danielle and Toby, the beautiful king and queen
To Labrier, a wise sage for us all
To my Mom, a wise sage for myself
And to Amiel, the wisest of all; may we all heed His council daily

"I know that you can and will make a good leader, if you will let
Amiel make you into one...a good leader always listens to the
council of his friends. While all final decisions rest in your hands,
remember to ask your friends for guidance, and they will gladly
give it.
Now, let us pray together."

~Christine E. Schulze

PART 1

CHAPTER 1

Five forms slinked from the girls' dorms to the boys'. Chasmira, Rachel, Hailey, Krystal, and Tiff cautiously rounded the corner and stopped before that familiar door. Chasmira knocked lightly.

From within Josh shouted, "Pizza's here!" while Sam hissed, "Go back to sleep, you idiot!" and Nathan sneered, "He *is* asleep—talking in his sleep again—"

Aaron slowly opened the door, muttering, "Come in..." before shuffling over to the big arm chair and flopping down.

"Thanks for the warm welcome," mumbled Krystal.

"This better be good," Josh warned, finally waking up. "I was having this dream about being chased by a chocolate-covered butterfly...and then there was this flying pizza..."

"It's a letter from Mrs. Daniels, and we couldn't wait until tomorrow to open it," explained Tiff.

Everyone suddenly sprang wide awake, crowding around Chasmira as she tore into it. They had been exchanging letters the past few months. It was summer, but they remained at school to squeeze in a couple of extra classes, sheer ludicracy in the boys' opinion, but they stayed on so "the girls wouldn't get lonely." Soon they would all turn eighteen, and once they received their magic powers, this would mean necessary extra classes to master those special abilities.

As Chasmira scanned the letter, face brightening, she took in a deep breath of awe.

"What's it say?" demanded Rachel.

"She says she's had her baby!" exclaimed Chasmira.

All the girls squealed and the boys rolled their eyes, except Josh who cried with unconcealed delight, "I'm an uncle!"

"Oh, wait. It says she's had twins!"

All the girls squealed again, Josh wildly shouting, "I'm like—like a double uncle!"

"It's a daughter, Mirabel Pallas, and a son, Cooper Jackson. Awe, there's no pictures..."

"There's this though." Aaron pulled from the envelope a blue, shimmering, strangely familiar stone.

"Oh, wait," said Chasmira. "It says 'I've enclosed Chasmira's warping stone. Come visit as soon as you can. I miss you all, and hope to see you soon.'"

"Awe, do we really have to," groaned Josh. "I mean, I'd like to see the kids and all, but I've been kinda liking having my sister gone—"

He grew abruptly silent as they all glared at him, Krystal rolling her eyes. "*Please*, you've been whining ever since she left."

"So what're we waiting for?" Aaron asked.

"It's Thursday night," Rachel reminded. "We have school tomorrow."

"I'm not afraid to skip classes."

"I don't think that would make Mrs. Daniels too happy," observed Hailey.

"Maybe not." Aaron shrugged. "But at least she can't give us detentions any more."

"True," agreed Tiff.

"Besides. We don't have to stay *all night*..."

He said it with a mischievous twinkle in his eye, but no one refused his idea. They all felt too eager themselves.

Together, they held hands and shouted, "To the Prismatic Isle!" Instantly, they were catapulted to another world.

How changed the Prismatic Isle appeared from the last time they beheld it. The beauty of its forests blossomed with fresh, teeming life. The soft moonlight cast a magical, almost angelic glow upon the landscape, which had transformed into rolling hills and lush, serene woods. They sidled towards the castle which stood only a few yards off and where the entrance guards warmly welcomed and permitted them.

They found Amanda Danielle in the garden beneath a ring of trees flourishing with glittering, white flowers. Humming softly, she cradled tiny Cooper in her arms while Mirabel slept soundly in her nearby stroller.

"Hey, sis!" Josh called and Amanda Danielle spun about in surprise. Then, upon seeing them all there, she beamed as brightly as the diamond flowers encircling her.

"Hello, it's so good to see you all. Although...I didn't expect you on a school night." Her eyes narrowed threateningly. "Homework's done, I hope?"

Chasmira smirked at Rachel who shared the same, knowing look. Mrs. Daniels may not have been their teacher any more, but the teacher still lived strongly inside of her, especially her bright blue eyes which gazed critically at the boys, particularly Josh.

"Oh, yeah, sure," Josh said rather quickly, casually shrugging his shoulders and avoiding his sister's sharp eye.

"Well, it *is* true," Nathan whispered to Aaron. "I mean, studying for that test isn't exactly homework...is it?"

"We came to see my new nephew and niece," Josh said brightly.

"They're so cute!" squealed Rachel while she and the other girls crowded around first Cooper then Mirabel. Both possessed soft, fair skin, traces of golden hair with rainbow highlights, and huge, round, inquisitive eyes that shone a striking blue, just like their mother's.

"Heh, heh, look at that," Josh announced proudly. "He's got my nose. Hey, Cooper. I'm your Uncle Josh. We're gonna have a great time together—ouch!"

Josh quickly recoiled as Cooper reached out and pinched Josh's nose.

"Yeah, he's got your nose alright," Krystal laughed.

Josh cast her a foul look, but the look quickly faded as his sister cast him one equally as sharply warning.

"I'm so glad you got to come and see them," she continued. "Toby's been show-ing them off to everyone he can. They're such a blessing, so well-behaved, and so fun to watch. Cooper has the funniest expressions. Always sticking out his tongue at Toby."

"Where *is* Mr. Daniels?" inquired Hailey.

"Important meeting." Amanda Danielle's eyes averted theirs ~~for a moment~~ to gaze at the stars. "He won't be able to see you tonight I'm afraid."

"That's alright," said Chasmira. "We have the stone. We can come visit again —"

"No!" Amanda Danielle snapped sharply, *eyes darting to them* and they all stared at her, shocked. Blushing at her own sharpness, she added, "Forgive me, I did not mean to shout so. But I do not think it would be a good idea for you to use your stone to come back here, not for a while. Please do not warp here anymore unless I ask you to, alright?"

"Okay," Chasmira said softly, though she and the others gazed at their beloved teacher with clearly confused expressions.

"Now, you should all be getting back. I don't want you to get in trouble or do badly on any of tomorrow's *tests*..."

As she cast another suspicious glance at the boys, Josh mumbled, "Freaky...how *does* she do it..?"

"...so I'll let you go, but not without a hug..."

So they all gave her a hug in turn. When Chasmira's turn came, she whispered into her ear, "Are you alright, Mrs. Daniels? Is something wrong?"

Amanda Danielle smiled and sighed. "No, dear, I'm just a bit tired lately. There's nothing to worry about."

Chasmira smiled in return but sensed something besides weariness in Amanda Danielle's eyes, though she could not read what that hidden expression meant.

The hugs all passed out, the students ~~all~~ took hands and said their final good-byes.

"See ya later, Mrs. D.," chirped Nathan cheerfully, hopping into the warp circle.

"Yeah, see ya, Sis," said Josh, following. "Keep the little squirts out of trouble for me while I'm gone."

"We can still write you, can't we?" asked Rachel.

"Of course."

"Good-bye, Mrs. Daniels," said Chasmira. "We love you."

After everyone shouted, "To Aaron's dorms in Lynn Lectim Academy!" and vanished, Amanda Danielle's smile faded and she finally allowed a tear to trickle down her cheek as more filled her eyes. "Yes," she said softly. "Good-bye, my children..."

CHAPTER 2

Months passed since their meeting with Amanda Danielle. They didn't forget that day. Indeed, they all thought Amanda Danielle's actions a little odd that night, not to mention the fact Josh was still going on asking why they shouted "Aaron's dorms". Why not "Josh's dorms?" It sounded totally cooler, couldn't they all tell? But at last they grew distracted by the prospect of a very special event—their first day of college.

The carriages rolled up to the tall, stately building. Its massive frame towered mansion-like as did the high school, only far larger and grander. As they pulled up, everyone was exiting *(exited)* the carriages, suit cases in hand, meandering around the campus grounds, looking for old friends and waiting for everyone to start piling inside.

From one particular carriage stepped three girls—Chasmira, Rachel, and Hailey.

"Woe," breathed Hailey. "Now *that's* cool."

"Hmm?" said Rachel. "Oh, the school. Yeah, I read that it—"

"No, no, the giant tree over there. It's so lofty."

Rachel sighed.

"Umm...you were saying?" Chasmira turned to Rachel.

"Ah, yes, I was reading—"

"Oh, hey, you must be Chasmira."

Rachel growled at this new interruption, but as she, Chasmira, and Hailey all wheeled around, they could only stare, dumbfounded.

Before them stood a tall, handsome fairy. His hair rippled a dark brown like milk chocalate, and his intriguing eyes flashed a dazzling shade of cerulean blue. And *he* was talking to *them.*

Chasmira suddenly realized that she must look very stupid gaping at him, so quickly closing her mouth and trying to put on a more serious air, she stammered, "And, umm...and who are you?"

"A person," replied the boy with a half-smirk. It really didn't help matters that his smile dazzled as well.

"Well, that's...informative..." mumbled Chasmira, who could feel by now she blushed profusely, rendered utterly powerless to cease the slow flow of crimson creeping across her cheeks.

"His name's 'Eric,'" explained a familiar voice. Aaron. He walked toward them, Nathan at his side, Sam and Josh following, though Sam seemed to be limping slightly.

"He went to Lynn Lectim Academy a couple years ago," Aaron added as the four boys joined the group.

"Dang, Aaron." Eric's half-smirk widening just a bit, strengthening its captivating pull. "I was about to tell them I was a secret agent or something."

"So, how do you know me?" asked Chasmira.

"Oh, Aaron talks about you all the time. About how you're the smartest girl in school, got highest grade average last year, graduated high school with honors..."

As Eric rattled on, Chasmira suddenly found interest in staring at the tree that Hailey was fascinated by only moments before. Perhaps because she turned a vibrant shade of red again.

As if noticing her friend's awkward state, Rachel cut in rather loudly, "So, Sam, what did you do to your foot?"

"Hmm?"

"Your foot—you were limping."

"Oh, that. Just a little accident with my pet fish this summer."

"Your pet fish?" Hailey asked, quite seriously, though Rachel and Chasmira found great difficulty containing their laughter, especially as Aaron performed a reenactment of Sam jumping around on one foot and screaming behind Sam's back.

"Yeah." Sam shrugged. "It's one of those glazeel piranhas. Jumped right out of the tank...Aaron's doing his reenactment again, isn't he?"

Chasmira nodded as Rachel burst out laughing.

Sam wheeled and Aaron quickly stood still, smiling. "What?" he asked innocently.

As Sam prepared to reprimand Aaron, Josh suddenly gaped and stared as though he'd just been bitten by a glazeel piranha himself. A familiar, vacant, droolworthy expression spread on his face as he breathed a familiar question, "Woah, who's she?"

In contrast to Josh's face, Aaron's flashed one of pure horror. "Oh, no. Oh no, no, *no*..."

"What's the matter with you two?" Krystal snapped, as she, Chasmira, Hailey, and Rachel all turned to see what the boys ogled at.

From one of the carriages stepped a beautiful, young Scintillate girl. Her glossy, strawberry blonde hair wisped about her in long, silky strands as the wind blew it, like magical sunbeams. Her crystal blue eyes seemed to be searching for something or someone. As her eyes fell upon their target, she revealed a dazzling smile that caused Josh's chin to drop just a little more.

To everyone's surprise, Chasmira suddenly shouted, "Sarah!" and dropped her suitcases on the ground (one landed on Josh's foot, smashing it, but he stood oblivious, still lost in his reverie), rushing over to the girl who at the same time surged with unparelled, swift grace towards Chasmira. When they reached each other, the girl dropped her suitcases as well and the two embraced.

"I'm so glad you came!" Chasmira exclaimed. "Why didn't you call?"

"Well, I wasn't *officially* coming until last week," admitted Sarah. "You know how fickle my mother can be." She rolled her eyes.

Chasmira laughed. Sarah's mom was defiantly the queen of last-minute decisions, and thus they usually referred to her as "the fickle-minded one."

"C'mon," said Chasmira. "I'll introduce you to everyone."

Sarah grabbed her suitcases and followed Chasmira over to the group of College Skylars, Josh still thoroughly enthralled in her beauty, Aaron looking as though he would rather be bludgeoned by a baseball bat than standing in her presence, and the rest looking confused yet curious.

"Hey, you guys, this is my best friend and pen-pal, Sarah," said Chasmira brightly.

"Hey, I'm Krystal."

"I'm Nathan. The guy with the enlargened toe is Sam."

"Yep, that's me...actually, it's 'enlarged—"

"Hailey. Nice to meet ya."

"Can I have your autograph?" Josh asked, getting right up in her face.

Sarah stepped back, glaring uncertainly at him. "Uhh...and I would do this *why*?"

"Aren't you that one famous model?"

"Umm...no..."

"Well, you sure are pretty enough to be one..."

Krystal grew very red and Nathan whispered to Sam that she was going to explode like a volcano if Josh didn't stop staring at Sarah. Rachel stepped between Josh and Sarah, pushing Josh away. "Josh, back off. You look like you're about to drool on her or something."

Rachel then smiled warmly at Sarah, adding, "Hi, I'm Rachel. Chasmira's told us all about you."

"It's nice to meet all—er—some of you..." Sarah cast uncertain glances at Josh.

"Hey, Sarah."

Sarah suddenly cringed and stiffened, looking up in the direction of the voice.

"Hello, Aaron," she said, somewhat coldly.

Aaron could tell this was not going to go well, but he could also tell how excited Chasmira was, so he may as well try to be civil for her sake.

"How's things going?" Aaron asked.

"Fine."

"Your family?"

"They're all...fine..."

"Well, that's...fine..."

"*So*," said Chasmira loudly, "we should head towards the school, right?"

"Yeah," agreed Rachel. "Looks like everyone's here and they're opening the doors..."

With suitcases in hand, they started for the school building. As they did so, Aaron walked up to Chasmira, hissing, "Why didn't you *tell* me she was coming?"

"I'm sorry," she whispered, "but I didn't know for sure."

"Well, you could've at least warned me or something. Evidently, she still hates me."

"She doesn't *hate* you, Aaron. Though...she *does* still refer to that incident you grabbed her hand and dragged her behind a bush in sixth grade, and she *does* still refer to you as 'that worm thing with the clammy hand' every now and then..."

"Well, whatever. What's past is past, and she needs to get over it."

"This isn't going to be one of those 'Rachel and Aaron' things, is it? I mean, I'm sure we won't be playing four square any more, but I don't want you two trying to knock each other out with your math books or something."

"Well, that *would* be a good use for them..."

"Aaron," she warned, casting him one of her classic, serious looks.

"I'm just kidding. There will be no book-throwing—unless *she* starts it," he added with a mischievous grin.

Rachel suddenly squeezed between Aaron and Chasmira, hissing at him, "Why didn't you tell me *he* was going to be here?"

"Who?" Aaron asked.

"*Eric Lindauer!*"

"Oh, you know him?" asked Chasmira. "He seems very nice."

"And very cute," Sarah added as she walked up besides Chasmira.

Rachel rolled her eyes. "Well, he went to Lynn Lectim the year before Chasmira came, and he was the most obnoxious kid in the whole school. He seems nice *now*, only because you've just met him, but, well, you'll see what I mean later on..."

"If he's so bad, why were you staring at him like the rest of us?" asked Chasmira.

"I—I was staring in horror," Rachel replied, as if not wanting to admit that she was just as enthralled by how his tall, handsome form had thoroughly grown out of its old, gangly self.

Passing into the entrance hall, they stared at the building's ornate and majestic beauty as well as its vastness. A wide marble staircase led upstairs to the classrooms. The girls' dormitories were housed on the next level, and the boys' dorms above that. Above them glistened a magnificent crystal chandelier and the windows were trimmed with fine silks. It was a very breath-taking first impression.

After being shown a room where they would leave their luggage so servants could come and take each person's bags to their rooms, they were told it was time to attend the grand, welcoming feast.

They were led to the dining hall, a far grander expanse than the one in Willard's mansion. It really seemed more like a cathedral with its high, arched windows, vaulted ceiling, ivory pillars, marble floor, and gold trimmings. Long banquet tables were arranged in neat rows throughout the room, the tables divided into sections. Each table was draped with a color representing their year. On the far left stretched tables covered in red for the Skylars(Freshmen), followed by turquoise for Lunars(Sophomores), orange for Solars(Juniors), and blue for the Celestials(Seniors). There were also three tables set end to end at the far end of the room, perpendicular to the students' tables. Seated at these tables were all the teachers and other staff.

Everyone took their seats, and an elderly, wise-looking man whose hair shimmered nearly white arose. A great hush fell across the room, and everyone's eyes focused upon him.

"Welcome," he greeted, his voiced projecting in a way that seemed foreign to his slim, anciently wrinkled form, "to another wonderful year at Lectim College, and as for our Skylars, I hope they have a wonderful first day here."

"What about the rest of the days?" asked Aaron.

"Sh!" hissed Rachel and Sarah in unison.

"I am Pastor Saltzgiver, Dean of Lynn Lectim and Pastor of the Lectim Chapel," continued the man. "And I'm sure I shall enjoy getting to know each and every one of you..."

Aaron noticed that as Pastor Saltzgiver talked, his eyebrows twitched sporadically up and down. The more he talked, the more rapidly his eyebrows seemed to jump. Aaron wanted to point this out to Chasmira, but feared he might burst out laughing right then and there.

"...also, for our Skylars, I'm sure you remember that your high school senior trip was canceled? It has been rescheduled, and shall take place the fifth week of school, during the teacher's convention when everyone else shall be on vacation—"

Loud cheers erupted from all tables, especially the Skylars', and Aaron took the liberty to burst out laughing. He ignored Sarah who gave him a very nasty look, as though he wasn't aloud such happiness.

"—Which shall include a ball which the gentlemen may invite the young ladies to—"

The girls looked quite pleased about this bit of news though the guys cast each other troubled glances.

"—Yes, so without further ado, let us thank Amiel for this bountiful feast, ask that He bless our school year, and begin!"

As soon as Pastor Saltzgiver prayed and asked the blessing, food heaped high and steaming hot suddenly appeared upon golden platters before them.

"Whoa," said Josh. "This beats the food line in high school."

"The food is brought out by fairies whose special ability is running lightning-fast," explained Rachel. "Remember learning about it in History last year?"

"I don't really care *how* the food got here." Nathan piled mashed potatoes onto his plate. "Let's just eat it."

"Well, excuse *me* for paying attention in History," Rachel snapped. "Just because *some* people only cared about the candy at the end of each lesson..."

"Speaking of special abilities..." Hailey turned to Aaron. "Shouldn't you have yours? Your birthday was this summer, right?"

"Yep. Ahh...special abilities," drifted a contented voice from where Aaron should be sitting, but he was no where to be seen. Then, the next instant, he sat visibly before them again.

"I know what *I'll* be doing during Math class," he added slyly.

Chasmira rolled her eyes. "Oh, of all things you would have to get invisibility. Could someone please pass me the—oh, never mind." As Chasmira stared at the fried chicken platter, it floated over to her, knocking Sam in the head in passing.

"Sorry. I'm still perfecting my levitation skills..."

"Man, you fairies are so lucky." snorted Rachel. "All we Forest-footers get is a suddenly-activated green thumb and toe...So, Sarah, what about you? You're a fairy. What's your special ability?"

"I can shape-shift," Sarah announced proudly, and suddenly her appearance changed to that of Rachel's. Changing back, she added, "My favorite is changing into my dog, Missy. Then I can actually be around her without her trying to bite me."

"Cool." Aaron smirked. "Though...wouldn't something like a fat toad fit you more appropriately?"

Chasmira looked away so as not to laugh—and in case Sarah suddenly attacked Aaron.

But Sarah merely replied coolly, "Well, you know the story of the frog turning into prince? I would therefore become a beautiful princess."

"Yeah, but who would kiss a toad—" Aaron's roast beef suddenly caught flame. He spotted Krystal glancing around innocently.

Aaron and Sarah passed the rest of the meal in stark silence. Everyone could sense the tension smoldering between them, and no one wished to encourage it, accidentally or otherwise. Especially no one wished for their own supper to catch ablaze.

The platters continued to magically refill until the hour-long feast ended, then everyone was shown to their rooms. The dorm rooms looked much like those of Willard's mansion, antique in style and furniture. Their luggage had all been stowed in each room, and everyone dispersed to their rooms to unpack and meet their new roommates.

Chasmira shared a room with Sarah, Rachel, and Krystal. Hailey, Kelsie, Tiffany, and Anyta shared a room right next to theirs. As soon as they were in the room and shut the door behind them, Sarah started venting, "I can't *believe* him! The *nerve*! A *fat toad*! I *never*! And you—you didn't even defend me, Cassy! I saw you turned away, laughing into your napkin."

"I wasn't," she said in a rather unconvincing tone, again stifling a chortle.

"You *were*," Sarah snapped. "You're doing it again, that—that quivery thing with your lips. Anyhow...a *fat toad*. And I'm not even fat...am I?"

"No, dear, you're lovely. Let's just unpack our bags and get settled. We all need a good night's rest."

As Sarah opened her suitcase, rather violently pulling her socks out and stuffing them into one of the drawers of the nearby chest, she mumbled, "A fat toad...I mean, a *fat toad*...that's just...a fat toad..."

After several minutes of silence, Krystal asked, "So, what exactly do you have against Aaron?"

"Oh, he's just annoying!" Sarah exclaimed and Chasmira cast Krystal a sarcastic "thanks-a-lot" look. "And there was that one time he did something to make me mad."

"Which is..?" Chasmira asked.

"Well—I don't remember at this moment in time. But that's beside the point."

"Didn't he grab your hand or something?" Rachel suggested, and Sarah cast Chasmira a look that said how dare she tell people such horrid things, but Chasmira's lips only twitched as she fought back another fit of laughter.

"Well," said Krystal. "*I* for one agree with you. I can't stand him either."

Krystal pulled out a small bottle from her backpack, rubbing some of its contents onto her arms and neck. The scent of mangoes filled the room.

"Mmm, that smells wonderful," said Sarah.

"It's the new lotion Josh got for me. It's called 'Exotic Mangoes.' I think he likes me." She smiled dreamily. Chasmira rolled her eyes. As if it was such a thrilling thing to be liked by the boy who crushed on practically every girl in their class during their senior year of high school.

The girls finished unpacking, and after brushing their teeth and pulling on their nightgowns, each climbed into the canopy beds and turned off the lamps set on night stands beside each bed. Krystal was the last to turn her lamp off. She took a half hour to brush her teeth, declaring she was trying to "perfect her smile for Josh". Then, as silence flooded the room, they each closed their eyes and drifted into dreamland.

CHAPTER 3

Chasmira was having the most pleasant dream. She and Aaron were on a cruise. She was dressed in a sparkling white gown, and he wore a handsome tuxedo. They were holding hands, walking on deck. They stopped to gaze at the stars, and then Aaron turned towards her, gazed into her eyes, and—

Chasmira was awakened by an ear-splitting scream. Thoroughly annoyed, she sat up to see Sarah and Rachel also sitting up, stretching and yawning and muttering irritably. Krystal was no where in the room, but a light shone from the bathroom.

"Krystal," groaned Rachel as she glanced at her watch. "This better be good. We're not supposed to be up for another hour."

Krystal suddenly wailed loudly from within the bathroom. Rachel rolled her eyes and slid from bed, Chasmira and Sarah following. *shuffling after.*

They entered the bathroom where Krystal slouched turned away, hands covering her face as she shook her head, moaning tragically.

"What's going on, Krystal?" Rachel asked groggily. "If you've only broken a nail again—"

"This is awful! I can't go to my first day of school looking like *this*!" Krystal cried.

"Well, you know, it's technically the *second* day," said Sarah, trying to sound comforting.

"Come on, show us what's wrong," said Chasmira. "It can't be *that* bad."

Krystal's voice suddenly changed to more of a spiteful growl as she turned. "I'm gonna *kill* Josh White." *morphed into*

Chasmira, Rachel, and Sarah were suddenly very awake. Krystal's neck and arms were covered in huge, bright purple pimples.

All they could do was stare, afraid of laughing or saying the wrong thing. Through the purple, Krystal turned red with rage.

"I'm gonna march to his room right now, and—"

Rachel and Chasmira grabbed her, holding her back.

"Now, we don't need you getting detention the first day at college," said Rachel. "I mean, the *second* day," she added as Sarah opened her mouth to correct her.

"Let's just find the hospital wing," suggested Chasmira. "I was checking my map. It's on the bottom floor."

"Let's get going then," sighed Krystal. "And let's hurry, because I think they're spreading."

Chasmira, Rachel, and Sarah all looked at each other but said nothing as several more pimples erupted on her nose.

* * *

Krystal's pimples were easily taken care of though the nurse looked quite despondent as they announced Krystal was given the pimple-causing stuff by Josh White.

"Oh, another White child," she groaned depairingly. "I can see now you'll be a regular..."

The girls afterwards made their way down to breakfast, all pimple-free, when Aaron, Josh, Nathan, and Sam suddenly rounded the corner. Josh was doing what looked like an impression of someone whose just discovered purple pimples erupting all over their face, and the other boys were busting up laughing.

"Not a word about this morning," whispered Krystal.

The boys noticed the girls approaching and quickly drew silent, trying to look serious, their faces a weird contortion of constrained laughter and strained solemnity.

13

"Good morning, ladies," greeted Josh. He nodded to each of them then turned to Krystal. "Did you try that new lotion I gave you?"

Nathan sniggered but tried to mask it with a fake sneeze. This proved altogether unsuccessful, but the girls pretended not to notice as Krystal replied, "Oh, yes, it was lovely."

Krystal smiled, enjoying the look that spread across Josh's face. He looked extremely disappointed and perplexed that her face was not covered in purple pimples. His face twisted into an odd, forced smile. "Oh...great..."

"By the way, I forgot that I got you something too," Krystal continued brightly, drawing a small box from her pocket. "It's this new hair gel. Turns your hair a surprise color."

"Awe, sweet!" Josh exclaimed, taking the box. "I'll try it on after breakfast. I hope my hair turns green..."

Krystal took his hand, and the couple led the way to the dining hall. As the others followed, Aaron whispered to Chasmira, "She knows about the lotion, doesn't she?"

"Oh, yeah."

"And she jinxed the hair gel, didn't she?"

"Without a doubt. Oh, and Aaron?"

"Yeah?"

"Don't ever give me something like that," Chasmira smiled, at the same time giving him a very warning glare.

Breakfast was wonderful, except for the fact that someone placed an ice spell on some of the pancakes. Sam was unfortunate enough to get one and his tongue turned to solid ice as he took a bite. As Krystal was carefully unthawing it, trying not to scorch the rest of his mouth, Rachel read the Daily Triangle, the college's newspaper, and suddenly exclaimed, "Oh, look! There's an article here about the high school. It appears they've found a new English teacher, Mr. Durg...he looks like a hippy from the seventies—Mrs. Daniels would be appalled. And—jikes! Mrs. Labrier's gone!"

"What?!" shouted Nathan, nearly choking on his cranberry juice. "She's quit?"

"No, she's gone—missing."

Everyone crowded around Rachel, straining to read the article.

"Mrs. Labrier—she was your History teacher, wasn't she?" asked Sarah.

Chasmira nodded, and then everyone drew silent as Rachel said, "Back off, people, I'll read it...It says here that 'Mrs. Labrier seems to have vanished in the middle of the night. She has left no trace or note to tell of her whereabouts. Consequently, History classes at the high school campus have been cancelled until further notice...'"

"Awe, nuts," said Aaron. "No one ever cancelled History while we were there..."

"What do you think it means?" asked Hailey. "You think someone's in trouble?"

"Something's got to be wrong." Chasmira frowned, glancing at Aaron. They were both thinking the same thing. His eyes always shared his deepest thoughts. Was Mrs. Daniels in some sort of trouble? She looked very worried when they last visited her long ago, not to mention a couple months passed since they received another let-

⚡ *Chapter breaks*

ter from her. As a queasy feeling gripped her, Chasmira hoped and prayed everything was alright...

CHAPTER 4

All of the Skylars were required to take general studies for the first half of the year. This meant everyone had to take a class in Math, English, History, and Science. They could also join the special ability clubs at this time. One of the clubs' purposes was solely to train all fairies and elves in the special abilities they were blessed with. Each fairy and elf was either born with certain magical powers or else received them at the age of maturity, eighteen. While they each naturally bore only one or two magical abilities, they could also join clubs to gain new ones though they would always be most skilled in their natural-born gifts. It had become an established law between the Fairy Council and the United States Government that all Fairies and Elves were required to partake in this special training for both purposes of mastery and the safety of non-magical peoples.

The joining of the clubs made everyone quite happy, especially Hailey and Rachel who soon grew frustrated with being Forest-footers. The only club for them was called the "Garden Club."

"Garden Club..." Rachel shuddered, "that sounds way too lame and girlish..."

So Rachel decided to join shape-shifting with Sarah, along the Water Club, while Hailey decided to join the Shrinking club which emphasized not only shrinking, but also enlarging. She quite enjoyed the name given to the members, the "Shrinky-dinks", and as she was a fast learner, soon became quite skilled, figuring out how to shrink herself and an entire comfortable living room set small enough to fit in a ~~small~~ *tiny* box. She determined she would mail herself home in this fashion for Christmas vacation that year instead of going by plane.

"Wouldn't it have been easier just to join the Warping Club and travel that way?" Sam inquired.

"Yep," Hailey replied matter-o-factly. "But not half as interesting."

Sam concurred this was true and decided to join the Shrinky-dinks as well, especially after Hailey informed him they would soon be practicing the enlargement of herbs.

Chasmira thoroughly enjoyed her levitation classes, almost as much as Aaron and Eric enjoyed their invisibility ones, if indeed Aaron enjoyed them too much.

Sam was walking down the hall one day and Chasmira followed a few feet behind him. They both treaded along silently, minding their own business, when a book soared through the air and whacked Sam in the head.

"Ouch!" he shouted, ~~turning~~ *wheel*. "Chasmira, that's a horrible way to practice your levitation skills—"

"It wasn't me!" she protested, though trying not to laugh.

~~Suddenly~~, someone burst out laughing close-by, and though they saw no one, Sam growled, "We know you're here, Aaron," just before dodging a pencil launched straight at his face.

Nathan took a simpler approach, completely content just to continue learning how to materialize food—his special ability was materialization and summoning, but he cared for materializing nothing save pizza and donuts and such—despite Rachel's constant, nagging, "You can do more!" speeches.

Tiff was skilled in healing inanimate objects, such as broken lamps or restoring the pencils Aaron was always chewing, while Krystal took fire lessons and Josh sought to perfect his lightning skills.

Krystal proved a fast learner too and could soon burn holes through walls. Krystal wasn't actually a Late-born, but now she had the opportunity to learn to better master and control her skills. Josh soon grew fearful, for all he could produce was a spark. What if he made Krystal angry, as he was so accustomed to doing, whether he meant to or not? How would he defend himself?

But the most fun classes of all were flying classes for the fairies who just gained their flying powers. Aaron, Sarah, and Josh caught on quickly, but Chasmira was a little slow with flying, namely because she was afraid of heights and feared plummeting from the sky. However, the others greatly encouraged her, and when she did fall, Eric always seemed to catch her just in time. Having received his flying powers at birth, he volunteered to help with the beginners. She always seemed to blush when he so artfully caught her, at least in Aaron's mind, but he shrugged it off. She would've blushed if any guy caught her, even Josh.

But the special ability clubs only occupied the afternoons. Regular classes must be endured during the morning. Thus Chasmira was muttering irritably to herself that first morning as she made her way down to Trig. Class. Everyone was required to take an advanced math class, so she chose Trigonometry, knowing Aaron was taking it too. How that would help her, she didn't know, as he hated math more than she did. But at least if they failed, they would do so together.

So she raced down the hall, mumbling how stupid it was that people such as herself, majoring in elementary school teaching and creative writing, had to take advanced math classes they would never use, and how over a thousand years had passed since the school's founding. Couldn't someone adjust the requirements by now? And the maps must be a thousand years old too, for they showed the Trig. Classroom as being located on the west side, not the east, and she was going to be late.

Finally, the Trig. room loomed into sight, and she rushed to it. Why didn't she choose an algebra course like Rachel and Hailey? At least then they could all be late together. How stupid she would feel walking in late on her own...

However, as she slowly opened the door and peered through, she was surprised. The room held enough desks for about fifteen people, but the only person there was Eric. Their professor wasn't even inside yet. Perhaps Caleb was wrong and the Trig. Room really *was* on the west side. Ooo, if he was playing a trick on her she would levitate an entire bookshelf into his head. Yet, surely Eric knew what he was doing—she hoped.

Chasmira took a seat to the left of Eric. He didn't even notice as she sat down. He sat thoroughly enthralled in a game he played on his calculator.

"Hey," she greeted and he looked up, smiling, and put the calculator down.

"Hey, Chasmira."

"Are we the only ones in Trig. Class—besides Aaron?"

Eric shrugged. "Aaron's *supposed* to be here, but he's late. Guess it doesn't matter though, since the professor's not here either. Dunno of anyone else in the class though."

After a pause, Eric said thoughtfully, "So...you're Chasmira..."

"Erm...yes," she said slowly.

"You don't look like I thought you would."

"What's that supposed to mean?"

"I—well, it's just that Aaron mentioned how pretty you were, but I didn't know you'd be so beautiful..." Eric suddenly glanced away, drumming his fingers anxiously on the desk.

Chasmira did not notice his face turned a vibrant shade of red, instead staring off dreamily.

"Aaron said I was pretty..?"

"Erm—"

The door suddenly slammed open and a breathless figure rushed in. Aaron stood in the doorway, staring at the two in confusion.

"Is this the right room?"

Eric shrugged. "According to the map."

"Oh, well." Aaron plopped in front of Chasmira. "If not, at least we've missed the first day of math, and we can blame it on the map."

"I hope we're in the right place. I don't want a detention on the second day of school..."

"Just because *you're* perfect and have never had a detention," teased Aaron.

"You've never gotten a detention?" Eric echoed.

"Well, not since sixth grade."

"Hmm..." A sudden, mischievous glint glimmered in his eye.

Chasmira glanced innocently from Eric to Aaron who also looked like he was up to no good, then back again.

"What?" she asked.

"Well, Eric and I made this deal that we would try to get all the students who've never gotten detentions at Lynn Lectim into detention this year," said Aaron.

"Why?" asked Chasmira, not liking the sound of this at all.

"For fun." Eric shrugged.

Chasmira glared at Aaron. "You wouldn't dare..."

Aaron smirked almost innocently.

"Do they even really have detentions in college though?" Chasmira asked.

"In this one they do," Eric said. "At least, that's what I heard."

"Of course we get the weird college with the retarded rules," mumbled Aaron.

Suddenly, the door creaked open again. They paid little attention, continuing to cast each other various glares (two were mischievous and the other threatening), until the person who entered said, "Sorry I'm late, guys."

At the sound of his voice, the three of them whirled.

"Mr. Root!" Chasmira exclaimed.

"No, way, he *can not* follow us to college," muttered Aaron.

"*He's bald*!" Eric gasped, gaping as he stared.
and staring

"Yes, it is Mr. Root, and he is bald," Mr. Root confirmed.

"What are you doing here?!" Aaron blurted, agitated. "Go back to the high school!"

Mr. Root smiled slyly as he walked to the lectern at the front of the classroom.

"Sorry, Aaron, but you're stuck with me again this year."

"What—how—?"

"I've been praying about being a math teacher for some time," Mr. Root explained. "However, I had to wait until Amiel prepared someone to take over my position as Principal at the high school. A young man arrived this summer asking to fulfill that position, and so here I am."

"But you're *bald*," Eric repeated, still gawking in utter disbelief.

"Ah, yes. Well, it seems there was a hurricane in Louisiana. Destroyed a school down there called Hope Academy. I told the high school students last year that if they could raise two thousand dollars over the summer for the school, I'd shave my head as a 'going-away' present for them."

"It took forever." Aaron rolled his eyes. "I've never seen such a slow head-shaving in all my life. Well...I've never seen *any*, but the point is that it was boring, sort of a rip-off."

"Well, the elementary school got to help too, and *they* enjoyed it thoroughly, especially my children," said Mr. Root.

He suddenly paused to glance about the room.

"My, but it is empty in here..."

Aaron closed his eyes as if wishing he would declare there were too few people to continue the class at all. This moment of hope turned out to be incredibly brief though, shattered with Mr. root's next words:

"...Well, let's get started."

They didn't learn a great deal from their Trig. books that day. Mr. Root was very easily distracted, and they spent half the class talking about gardening. It all started when Aaron asked, "How do pineapples reproduce if they don't have seeds?" By the time the bell rang, they discussed everything from giant tomatoes to invisible grapes. Chasmira grew thoroughly annoyed with this distraction and eventually blocked out the conversation, finishing her Trig. homework before the class was over. It proved not to be that difficult after all.

As they left Trig., Aaron asked Chasmira, "So, what's your next class?"

"English 102."

"102?" he and Eric echoed, staring.

"What happened to 101?" asked Eric.

"I passed out of it. Rachel too."

As she hurried down the hallway past them, they shook their heads, Aaron muttering, "Some people are too smart for their own good..."

"Detention..." reminded Eric.

* * *

Rachel and Chasmira were delighted to discover they shared English not only with each other but with Sarah as well. They were yet further delighted to find they all attended Geography together right after English.

English passed quickly. Mr. Lund, their teacher, was a very witty Forest-footer and thus possessed a good sense of humor. They accomplished little but reading the syllabus and talking about the great essay they would be writing that semester, more people complaining than actually talking about it, accept, of course, for Rachel, Chasmira, and Sarah. Rachel loved writing almost as much as she did reading. Sarah wasn't the greatest of writers when it came to punctuation, grammar, and form, but her mind was always loaded with ideas for things to write, and besides, Chasmira could always proofread it. And Chasmira, while studying to be a teacher as were the other two girls, also desired to become a writer, and thus thrilled at the thought of writing a paper.

Moving on to Geography, they found themselves sharing that class with Josh and Krystal who said little, constantly in the process of casting each other suspicious glances.

Sarah, Rachel, and Chasmira sat on the other side of the room, away from the odd couple. After glancing around and commentating to each other about the girls with the fro, as well as the sleeping guy, whom they confirmed must be a distant relative of Caleb, they turned their attention to the door as it opened, and in zipped a Mira man wearing glasses and a pink polo shirt, his dark hair spiked. Setting his briefcase on the desk, he leaned over the desk and greeted with a wild, over-enthusiastic gleam in his eye, "Welcome to *World Regional Geography*. I'm Mr. Arnolds. Are you guys ready to learn about the coolest subject ever?"

The class replied only with blank stares, uncertain what to make of the eccentric fellow.

"*Oh, yeah*," said Mr. Arnolds dramatically before pulling down a map of Africa.

Mr. Arnolds could soon be described as quirky yet enthusiastic, and above all, his class proved anything but dull. Sarah ventured that he was a hippy-wanna-be. At intervals, he would pause in his teaching to sniff the map, inhaling deeply as if smelling his favorite kind of pizza, and he would, from time to time, hold the chalk between two fingers and set it to his lips as if smoking a cigarette. He also amused them by making animal noises when talking about the country's native wildlife, even the animals which didn't even have noises. He conjured a certain kind of whistling noise for the giraffe.

Only Sarah maintained a straight face, simply for the sake of seeing how he would react. Inside, she was cracking up. Not laughing proved a difficult thing to do, as Rachel sat on one side of her, about to roll off her seat in laughter, snorting occasionally, and as Chasmira, on her other side, laughed so much that by now she was hiccupping.

In the midst of all this hubbub, sleeping guy (by name, Mr. Park) decided just to get up and walk out of the class as Mr. Arnolds was teaching. After a couple seconds, the teacher asked, "Dude, like, where did he go? Be right back..."

He zipped out of the classroom, and after a few moments zipped back in, shaking his head and smirking.

"Yeah, that guy who just left went one way down the hallway, paused, smiled and waved at me, then went the opposite direction down the hall like he was lost or something. Man, if you're going to skip class, at least know where you're skipping too...huh, what a freak..."

Everyone laughed but Sarah who just stared at him like he was crazy, throwing him quite off guard. He proceeded to stare at her with a wondrous expression.

Josh suddenly hopped from his seat and rushed from the classroom, shouting, "I'll get you, Krystal!" He was clutching what appeared to be a clump of his hair in one hand. The hair that remained was turning pink and falling out as well. A great bald spot already gaped on his head.

"Woah, what a freak!" Mr. Arnolds exclaimed. It was becoming very apparent that "freak" was his favorite word.

Krystal smiled to herself in a very pleased sort of way and Sarah leaned over to Chasmira and whispered, "Do they *really* like each other?"

Chasmira shrugged. "It's a love-hate relationship."

Class soon ended, sadly, and as they all filed out, Chasmira asked Krystal, "What did you do to him?"

"Hair gel." She smirked.

Chasmira shook her head, then turned to Rachel and Sarah. "I have an hour off before lunch. Want to do something?"

"Can't." Rachel shook her head. "Biology."

"Me too," said Sarah. "Music, that is."

"Very well then, see you at lunch," Chasmira announced as the two raced off to their next classes.

As Chasmira walked casually down the hall, she spotted Hailey and Sam hurrying towards her and raced to catch up with them.

"Hey, you two," greeted Chasmira.

"Hey," said Hailey absent-mindedly. Neither she nor Sam slowed their pace or stopped.

"Do you guys have class right now?" Chasmira asked.

"No," said Sam shortly.

"Would you like to hang out in the gym or something?"

"We have no time for childish games. We're going to the garden to study herbs."

"Studying to be doctors," Hailey added. "We don't learn about herbs until our second year, but you can never start too early, you know."

Chasmira came to a halt and watched as they zoomed out of sight. She smiled then sighed, deciding she may as well make for the library before heading off to lunch.

CHAPTER 5

Aaron and Eric complained of having to write about fast food, Rachel announced how biology was disgusting and contained entirely too many dead frogs for her liking, and Sarah muttered about the piano in their music class being very off-key and thus messing up her singing. Aaron wondered aloud if it was not just her voice that was messed up which instantly got his roast beef reduced to cinders again, and he scowled at Krystal as she smiled in a pleased sort of way.

"*So*," Sarah said loudly, trying to get everyone's minds off the terrible classes, "I don't think I heard what all you guys' majors are. I know me, Chasmira, and Rachel are teachers, and Krystal and Tiff are doing some fashion design stuff and whatnot, but what about you all?"

"Not sure yet," said Eric.

"Me neither," agreed Josh.

"Or me," declared Nathan.

"How shocking," mumbled Rachel.

"I'm thinking about being a playwright. I've started writing one already," Aaron explained. "Or perhaps a director. Something to do with film, you know."

"That's cool," Tiff remarked.

"And Hailey and I are both studying to be doctors." Sam drew himself up proudly, and Hailey nodded her head overenthusiastically, like one of those toys whose bobbing head is going haywire.

"Well, glad I'm not the only writer in the bunch," Chasmira smiled at Aaron.

"You like to write?" mused Eric.

"Yes, I've written loads of stories already. You could read one sometime if you like."

"Sure," he agreed eagerly, and as she smiled, his heart leapt towards her. How on earth would he ever be able to ask her to the ball..?

* * *

School had been in session for a couple weeks, and with the third week came the anticipation of two important events—the first Hoverball game that Monday evening and the senior trip to take place in two weeks.

Chasmira grew accustomed to having nothing to do in between History and lunch, enjoying the extra time to study, write, or read. But today she was in the mood for none of these things. She stirred restlessly about tonight's game. She felt even more restless about the cruise, and most restless about the ball. Would anyone ask her? Josh already asked Krystal. Sam was taking Hailey, "just as friends," of course. Even Nathan, who was usually such a scatterbrain about remembering important occasions, claimed Rachel. But would anyone—that is, would *Aaron*—ask her?

Swinging her backpack onto her shoulders, she decided to wander down to the garden. After all, the last time she visited there was last school year.

The phoenix clearing yet awaited her. She smiled at all the memories she accumulated there in just a few short months, as if standing in her most sacred treasure trove. This was where she gave Aaron the phoenix feather. Did he still keep it after all this time? This was also where Amanda Danielle took them to the Council of Spectrum, giving each of them the medallions. She reached into her backpack and touched it. Amanda Danielle told them to keep the medallions close always, and so she did. Finally, this was where Amanda Danielle and Toby hosted their wedding reception. It was such a magical place, staunchly alive with so many brilliant memories. She only wished one more memory could be created here. After all, it *would* be a bit romantic if Aaron asked her to the ball right here in the clearing…

Wandering through the garden, she came to the orchards. Picking an apple, she munched on it thoughtfully. The apples seemed especially good this year, and she found herself thinking how Aaron would probably like an apple. She picked the biggest, shiniest green apple she could find, slipping it carefully into her backpack.

As she prepared to leave the garden, a girl ~~suddenly~~ exclaimed, "Hoochy-wa!" and a guy cried with unconcealed drama, "*Oh, my goodness!*"

Stepping into a small clearing, she found Hailey and Sam staring up at a purple, swirly vine hanging from one of the trees.

"*Look!* At that herb," Sam inhaled sharply, clearly awestruck. "Have you ever *seen* such an herb?"

Chasmira quickly backed away so they wouldn't hear her laughing, quickly departing from the garden to leave them to their herbal privacy.

CHAPTER 6

The first Hoverball game of the year arrived. Everyone gathered in the stadium. Chasmira and Sarah sat about halfway up the stadium, anxious to watch Nathan's and Hailey's team, the Jades, face off against Rachel's, Tiff's, and Krystal's team, the Flamingoes. Sam didn't join any of the teams, and Aaron, Eric, and Josh were all on the Phoenix team so they wouldn't be playing that night. "Ought to be interesting," declared Sarah as she sat beside Chasmira, piling popcorn into her mouth. "Seeing Rachel against Nathan."

"Yeah, they're actually pretty competitive. At least, they were in high school games."

"And there's no annoying people to bother us. You *did* say the other guys were in their dorms studying, right?"

"Erm…right," Chasmira replied in a very unconvincing tone. She highly doubted the boys, especially Aaron, would really miss the whole game, not to mention free food, for homework.

Sarah either did not notice the unconvincing tone or else hopefully ignored it. "Good. It's bad enough having Aaron around. Josh though—if he stares at me *one more time*. I'd take Aaron over him any day…"

Pastor Saltzgiver ~~suddenly~~ walked onto the field, ~~and~~ after a quick announcement, a prayer, and a few eyebrow twitches, he left and the two teams flew onto the field, the elves flashing their silver, winged boots. The crowds erupted with cheers, waving either pink or green banners, and when the excitement subsided somewhat, the game began.

Things started out very slowly, with Nathan and Rachel fighting continuously for the ball. Finally, the coach announced they better pass the ball to their other members, and if they wanted to play a two-player game they could leave and join the chess club. After this was settled, a rough, competitive game ensued ~~that kept the~~ crowd wincing or flying to the edge of their seat and which kept Sarah saying, "Ooo, that had to hurt."

~~Suddenly,~~ Chasmira's eyes widened as someone climbed up the steps towards them. It was Josh.

Quickly, she looked away—surely Sarah would have a fit if she noticed him—but all too late. He looked up, immediately spotting her, smiling, and called, "Hey, Cass! Hey, Sarah! How's it going?"

Sarah's head snapped around and she stared at him as if he were a hideous ghost before turning her attention back to the game and mumbling, "Just fine before you showed up."

"Sarah, be nice," hissed Chasmira.

"Hmph."

"Can I sit here? Thanks." Josh plopped down besides Sarah before he could give her a chance to reject him.

Chasmira snorted, nearly laughing. Of course Josh wouldn't sit in one of the two empty seats next to her. She glanced at Sarah then looked away for fear of bursting out laughing. Sarah looked livid, lips tightly pursed, eyes fuming, her fair skin deepening to a dangerous crimson.

The Flamingoes scored another point, but Sarah, Josh, and Chasmira paid little heed. Chasmira suddenly wondered if Aaron would show up too, and Sarah was about ready to slap Josh as she felt his eyes boring into her, mesmerized by her beauty.

Finally, she turned and cast him such a death glare that he jumped as if she really punched him, then he said, "Uh—uh—I need more popcorn. Be back."

He sprang up off the seat, taking his half-full bag of popcorn with him and hurrying from the aisle.

"Thank Amiel," Sarah muttered, looking over at Chasmira who was ready to explode with laughter.

"Oh, for Pete's sake, let it out. I certainly don't think it's so funny though—"

"Hey, Aaron!"

At the sound of someone calling his name, two very different responses were instigated in the girls. Sarah stared straight in the direction of the game with wide, horrified eyes, turning redder every moment while Chasmira began looking around excitedly for Aaron. Instantly, she spotted him and Sam climbing the stairs, and hopping from her seat, raced down to meet them.

"Aaron!" Chasmira cried, nearly tripping down the stairs.

"Oh, hey, Cassy," Aaron beamed. "That was a really good apple."

For a moment, Chasmira stared at him in confusion, but suddenly remembering, she blushed a more brilliant shade than Sarah.

"Oh! The apple I gave you. It was good?"

"Very good," Aaron said, far more enthusiastically than anyone should talk about apples in Sam's opinion, as revealed by his sly smirk.

"That's good," said Chasmira.

This comment was followed by an awkward pause in which Aaron and Chasmira stood blushing as if trying to grasp something to say which did not involve the word "good", and in which Sam's inward smile tugged at the corners of his mouth, threatening to come out.

"So…uhh…is there room for us to sit with you?" Aaron asked.

"Sure." Chasmira's heart danced, yet at the same time she laughed inwardly, musing how Sarah would surely kill her. First Josh, now these two…

As Chasmira led them back to her row, Sarah's face and widened eyes flashed fierily before she turned back to the game, looking very perturbed, her lips pursed so

23

tight only the thinnest line remained. Chasmira forced herself from laughing as she sat next to Sarah. Aaron plopped beside her and Sam on the end.

"So how's the game going?" Aaron asked.

"Oh, erm…" Chasmira really hadn't been paying attention at all to the game.

"The Flamingoes are winning by a point," Sarah replied coolly, struggling to contain her annoyance.

"Oh, sorry, Sarah, didn't see you there. Hi," greeted Aaron.

Sarah forced a fake smile in his direction before snapping her attention to the game.

"So, did I mention I liked the apple?" Aaron asked, after a few minutes.

"I think you did," Chasmira returned, smiling. She'd never quite seen him like this before, so excited and almost nervous. Of course, she shared these feelings herself, though she felt sure his heart couldn't be pounding as hard as her own.

"Yeah, it was really good," Aaron said again.

"Was it as red as you two's faces?" Sam whispered, and Aaron jabbed him hard with his elbow. Sam didn't seem to mind though. He quite enjoyed himself, continuing to smirk in a proudly pleased way as the game progressed.

As they watched on in silence, the Flamingos scored two more points. Sam and Sarah clapped and cheered. So did Aaron and Chasmira, though with less enthusiasm and heart. They both sat distracted, desperately trying to think of something to talk about besides apples.

Chasmira jumped as Aaron asked abruptly, "So, did you see 'March of the Penguins?'"

"Oh, yes. I liked it."

"I thought it was sad. All the penguins getting eaten, starving, freezing to death…'

"Yes, Mom didn't like that either."

"Can I see that?" Aaron pointed to her notebook.

"Sure." She handed him both paper and pencil.

Chasmira watched as he began to draw, and Sarah couldn't help her eyes from straying over to the paper as well, intrigued.

"How cute!" she squealed. "A penguin. Can you draw a fox?"

"Sure."

As Aaron set to work, Chasmira cast Sarah a mischievous look, and Sarah squinted her eyes so as to say that, yes, reluctantly perhaps he wasn't *so* bad. At least he had courtesy to say "hi," but Chasmira shouldn't expect her to be *too* friendly. All this was exchanged with looks only. Chasmira sighed. That was the way of things. If you were around someone for so long, their thoughts scarily became your own…

The game progressed in silence between them, save for their cheering as the Flamingos scored another point.

Chasmira jumped as Aaron blurted, "Chocolate."

"What?"

"I feel I want some chocolate. Can I get you anything?"

"Erm…no thanks," she replied, her stomach performing far too many flip-flops for her to consider eating at the moment.

"We'll be right back then. Come along, Sam."

24

As he and Sam headed down the stairs, Sarah mumbled, "Finally, a few moments of peace."

~~Chasmira noticed~~ But Chasmira she studied the fox picture, and smiled ~~though~~.

For a few minutes, it actually *was* quite peaceful, and then—

"Hey!" Josh greeted, and Sarah nearly choked on her popcorn in repulsion, often unmasked as she looked over to see not only him, but Eric approaching as well.

"Look who I found at the popcorn stand," Josh ~~continued~~, resuming his previous position beside Sarah who looked very much like exploding by now. First Josh, then Aaron, now Josh, Eric, and soon Aaron all at once…the horror…

"No one's sitting here, right?" ~~Eric asked, and~~ before Chasmira could protest, Eric plopped down right beside her.

Josh had learned his lesson and didn't stare at Sarah this time. He did, however, offer her some popcorn, but after she called him a moron and hissed, "Can't you see I still have half a bag full?" he decided to give up and slouched back in his seat, mumbling, "Yeash, offer a girl some popcorn and she goes all defensive…"

Presently, Aaron and Sam returned, each carrying a mound of sweets, ~~and~~ as Aaron stared at Eric, wondering how and when and why he was sitting in his seat, Eric greeted cheerfully, "Oh, hey Aaron. Done studying already? Have a seat," before returning his attention to the game.

"Umm…hey…Eric," he murmured, all the while looking at Chasmira who gazed up at him helplessly, ~~and~~ understanding, Aaron rolled his eyes and ~~slouched~~ jumped down beside Eric while Sam sat behind Aaron.

After several minutes, Eric announced, "Awe, man, empty already. Be right back." Jumping up, he made off with the empty popcorn tub while Aaron hopped over to his seat next to Chasmira, and, smiling, held out a chocolate muffin. "Muffin?"

"Thanks," she smiled, taking the muffin and proceeding to eat it very slowly and carefully. This was one muffin, as well as one night, she wanted to take the proper time to savor.

Eric returned shortly, his popcorn already half-empty, though he only purchased it moments ago. Sarah commented ~~to herself~~ about him eating too much junk food, and surely he would die at thirty of a heart attack if he kept on that way. Eric ignored her, just staring at Aaron as if in great disappointment that he took the seat next to Chasmira, then plopped on the end beside him. Aaron seemed not to even notice he returned. His mind was too consumed with what he planned to do that night.

Eric's mind soon grew preoccupied as well. He abandoned Trig. Homework to come to this game for a very specific reason. There was something he very much wanted to ask Chasmira, though he knew it would must wait until after the game, and even then, he wondered if she wouldn't say "yes." After all, she didn't know him for very long at all…

As the game halted for half time, Aaron leaned over to Chasmira and whispered, "Cassy, I have to talk to you. Meet me in the garden after the game?"

"Of course." Her heart bounced as she imagined hopefully what he might want to talk about.

In the end, the Flamingos won, ~~and as~~ all the Flamingo fans rose to cheer, Josh waving his tub of popcorn excitedly, dumping popcorn all over Sarah who gave him a very dangerous glare. Aaron motioned to Chasmira and she followed him down the stairs.

Eric watched curiously as they left but wasn't worried. Surely, they would come back to the gym for refreshments and he could speak to Chasmira then.

Finally, Aaron and Chasmira escaped the noise of the celebrating stadium and entered the garden. As usual, the moon bathed everything in a magical, milky light. Chasmira smiled as he led her into the phoenix clearing wondrously illuminated by the moon.

Aaron glimpsed about, grinning. "So many memories…do you remember the time I told you I felt this would be special place for us someday?"

Chasmira nodded, beaming. How could she possibly forget?

"Well, it certainly has become special. So much has happened here. That's why I brought you here…to ask…"

As his voice trailed, Chasmira timidly looked up at him. He turned away shyly, and his face bright red. It was an awkward moment. After all, wasn't *she* supposed to do all the blushing? Both knew what wanted to be said, yet neither seemed to be able to utter the words.

Suddenly, at once they both took a deep breath, Aaron asking, "Would you go to the senior ball with me?" and Chasmira saying, "I'd love to."

Then they laughed, instantly feeling relieved.

"Really?" Aaron's face shone. "Do you really want to?"

"Yes." Chasmira's eyes glittered, dancing, laughing themselves as she did giggled lightly. "I'd go with no one else."

Chasmira and Aaron returned to the gym for refreshments, quite elated and quite hovering at each other's side the whole time. Consequently, though he searched for the right opportunity all night, Eric never got his word with Chasmira.

* * *

"I've done it!" Aaron exclaimed, rushing into his dorm room and shutting the door behind him.

"I've finally asked Chasmira to the ball."

Josh, Sam, and Nathan all looked up at him, grinning.

"Congrats, dude," said Josh.

"Indeed, yes," agreed Sam.

"Good for you," added Nathan. "Hope you didn't sweat and stutter as much as I did though when I asked Rachel. She was worried I was having a nervous breakdown or something…well, I probably *was*…"

Just then, Eric entered and Josh announced, "News flash, buddy. Aaron asked Chasmira to the ball."

Eric tried very hard to conceal the look of shock and hurt spreading upon his face. No one seemed to notice as he said quietly, "I suppose she said 'yes.'"

Nathan rolled his eyes. "Well, duh. She and Aaron have been friends for ages, and everyone's known for forever she has a possible thing for him. Who else would she go with?"

Eric flopped down on his bed, staring at the ceiling as Sam inquired, "And what about you, Eric? You asking anyone?"

For a few moments he did not reply, but when he did, his voice was low, as if he suddenly grew very tired, "No, I don't think I am…"

He sighed deeply as the boys rattled on, talking amongst themselves, oblivious of his pain. He missed his chance, and no one else existed in all the world that he would ever desire to take.

CHAPTER 7

The girls woke up excitedly next Saturday for the coming of school pictures dawned at last.

Rachel, Sarah, and Chasmira prepared their clothes and jewelry, adding some final, primping touches while Krystal lingered in the bathroom. She already spent a half hour longer than usual fixing her hair and was yet enthusiastically spritzing hairspray.

Finally, she emerged, smiling and holding something in her hand.

"See the new earrings Josh got me?" She showed them a pair of tiny diamonds shaped like hearts.

"I'm going to wear them today."

"Umm...do you think that's wise?" Chasmira raised a skeptical brow. "After the whole 'lotion' incident?"

"Oh, today's picture day," Krystal returned. "He wouldn't *dare* mess *that* up…"

Chasmira and Rachel cast each other more-than-uncertain glances.

Krystal donned the earrings, and Chasmira, Rachel, and Sarah all waited for her ears to explode or something, but nothing happened. Perhaps Josh honestly gave her a nice, normal gift this time.

Chasmira was pulling her silky pink dress over her head when she suddenly tripped, nearly falling over.

Krystal raised her brow. "You okay?"

"Sure…"

As Chasmira continued to stare dreadfully at her, Krystal asked slowly, "Is something wrong?"

"Umm…your ears—"

The words barely slipped from her mouth before Krystal rushed into the bathroom. She soon zoomed out, looking utterly petrified, shouting, "When I find Josh! Quick, we've got to get to the nurse and get this fixed right away…"

Rachel and Sarah gawked at Krystal as she hopped around, hurriedly trying to pull on her pantyhose. Krystal's ears were swelling fast. They were already twice their normal size.

However, when they reached the nurse, she announced glumly that Krystal's ears would not return to normal until—

"Tomorrow?! But we have pictures *today*!"

"I'm sorry, Miss Smith. There's nothing more I can do."

As the nurse walked off, Krystal scowled. "Josh *knew*, he *knew* I'd want to wear them for pictures…"

"Oh, it's not so bad," assured Rachel. "Maybe they won't all fit in the picture and no one will see…"

"But I can't let everyone see me like this!"

"You're just lucky it's Saturday and we don't have classes," Chasmira pointed out, Krystal's head really might not fit through the narrow doorway of her History class.

Krystal's face ~~suddenly~~ lit up as though she received the most enlightening idea. "Sarah, can I ask you a favor?" Her ears bloomed nearly as big as her head now, the earrings all but swallowed by them.

"Sure."

"Could you...do you think you could turn into me and take my picture for me?"

"What?!" Sarah's face flashed a sudden, vivid red. "No way. I am *not* getting involved. What if I get caught?"

Chasmira smirked slyly. "You know what Aaron would say. 'There's nothing in the school rules that says you can't do it.'"

"Actually, he'd be more like, 'Who cares if it's in the rules or not, just do it any-ways,'" corrected Rachel. "But Chasmira's right. It's not against school policy. You could always say you were just practicing shape-shifting anyways."

Sarah flipped her glossy red hair over her shoulder and returned in a mock-haughty voice, "I do not *need* practice. I am a perfect shape-shifter."

Rachel threw a pillow at her head, and Sarah laughed lightly. "Alright, alright, I'll do it. But certainly not because of anything *Aaron* said."

* * *

Sarah—in Krystal form—walked briskly down the hallway. She tried to mimic Krystal's walk—short steps, chin high, smiling at every boy she passed, always flipping her hair over her shoulder or glancing at her appearance in her compact mirror. But this soon got her nowhere until she had only ten minutes left to get to the dining hall where the pictures were being taken. She took to zooming down the hallways at a fast walk, causing many heads to turn and stare at confusedly. Sarah smirked, for she could guess their thoughts: What had gotten into Krystal? Wasn't she worried such brisk walking would mess up her hair or cause her to break a heel off? Or was she on her way to murder Josh for something?

As Sarah rounded a corner, she ~~suddenly~~ stepped back and flattened herself against the wall. She almost stumbled upon a conversation that Mrs. Miner and Pastor Saltzgiver muttered in quick, hushed tones:

"Pastor Saltzgiver, I understand, but do you think it's wise to let the children go on the cruise when there have been so many strange storms ~~in the ocean~~ lately?"

"Mrs. Miner, I can assure you that the *Coral 3* is the safest ship on the ocean. It's protected by magic so that it can't be affected by storms."

"*Normal* storms, yes, but what about dark magic..?"

It ~~suddenly~~ occurred to Sarah she was eavesdropping, and though utterly curious to hear the rest of the conversation, she quietly slipped down the hall and made a detour to the dining hall.

Sarah almost had to run the rest of the way, but when she finally got there, everyone stood in a line running around the ~~complete~~ perimeter of the room. On the raised platform where the teacher's tables usually were, a grey background was set up, and at the foot of the platform, several photographers set up their cameras and other equipment.

Sarah quickly found Chasmira, Hailey, and Rachel. "What's going on? Shouldn't they have started by now?"

"Well, yes." Hailey frowned. "But the photographers are dunderheads."

Sarah laughed. "What do you mean?"

"Let's just say there was an incident with one of them getting tangled in the wires of his equipment," said Chasmira.

"It was hysterical," chuckled Rachel. "You should've seen it."

"Anyways, they're almost ready, and they said we're doing group pictures first."

Sarah stared. "Group pictures? I hadn't even considered that. How am I supposed to pull that one off?"

Hailey grinned impishly.

"I've an idea…"

Soon they all piled onto the platform. Sarah stood next to Hailey, and Hailey took off one of her earrings and handed it to Sarah, who immediately shape-shifted it into a miniature version of herself. Hailey then enlarged it to Sarah's size. They completed this all so fast and there were so many people crowding for a good spot that no one really noticed, and the two smiled, admiring their work.

"Awe, man, look," Josh whispered, elbowing Nathan and pointing up at the fake Sarah as they passed below. "Sarah Schnur—staring right at me…"

"Get real," Nathan hissed, rolling his eyes and pushing Josh along.

Sarah growled, eyes seething. "If he even comes to me later thinking I like him…Krystal soooooo owes me…"

The group pictures soon completed, Hailey got her earring back and then they were told to form a line around the perimeter of the room as before, and one by one they filed up to get their pictures taken.

As the girls waited, Aaron suddenly came up to them bearing a quite agitated scowl. Chasmira noticed too he wore his dark brown sweater. He looked so handsome in sweaters, especially that one…no, she must not think such blush-worthy truths…

"What's wrong?" She really hoped the blushing wasn't too obvious.

"That photography guy is *so weird*—totally messed up my picture! Not that I like having my picture taken anyways…"

"What did he do?" asked Rachel.

"I had my smile just right. It was perfect. And right before he takes it, instead of saying, 'Say cheese,' or something else generic, he's like, 'Say fuzzy pickles.' If that doesn't disturb you and mess up your smile, nothing will. I mean, *'fuzzy pickles*?' We're in college, for crying out loud…"

The girls couldn't help but laugh.

"It's *not* funny…"

"What's not funny?" Josh suddenly strolled up beside Aaron. He gave the girls no time to answer though for he suddenly stared at Sarah with a confusedly twisted face.

"Krystal? What're you doing here?"

"Umm…having my picture taken?" Sarah returned.

"Oh." He stared at her for a while, cast a disappointed glance at her earrings, then sauntered off, mumbling how he ought to sue the person who kept selling him crummy prank gifts that never seemed to work.

"Well, I should go finish my homework," Aaron announced. "See you all later."

He started off and they all bid him good-bye. ~~Suddenly, though~~ he turned. *But then* "Hey, Cassy?"

"Yes?" Again her cheeks flamed.

"Umm…can you meet me in the garden later. Like, after lunch?"

"Oh, sure."

Aaron smiled and left. Chasmira grinned and sighed deeply.

Sarah smirked at her mischievously. "I wonder what that's all about? Do I smell…*love* in the air?"

"Oh, don't be silly," snapped Chasmira, blushing more furiously than ever.

"Well, it's *about time* he took notice of you," Sarah continued. "You've only been swooning over him since sixth grade."

"Oh, hush. You don't even like him."

"Well, he's not so annoying now. I can tolerate him."

~~Suddenly~~, someone droned behind them, "Ahem…ahem…ahem…"

Chasmira slowly turned her head towards Eric who smiled playfully. "I like saying the word 'ahem.'"

"You see what I mean about being annoying?" Rachel hissed while Sarah rolled her eyes. She then stifled a laugh, for Rachel was now the one blushing madly.

Chasmira bit her lip, also trying desperately not to laugh, so Rachel sighed loudly in frustration while Sarah leaned over and whispered, "Like I was saying, I can tolerate Aaron, but I don't think Rachel could *ever* tolerate Eric…"

"Don't be so sure." Chasmira nodded towards Rachel. As Eric looked in the opposite direction, Rachel gazed dreamily at him.

Sarah and Chasmira cast each other an all-too-well-knowing glance and forced down another giggle.

CHAPTER 8

for a good half hour

The four girls ~~were~~ *studied* in their room, along with Hailey. Sarah had taken to humming love songs. Finally, Hailey shot up into sitting position, exclaiming, "Hoochy-wa! That's enough! I can't take it anymore! Do you have to keep up that incessant humming?!"

"No worse than you humming the 'Charmin Ultra' commercial ~~music~~ *song*," Rachel commented.

"Yes, and at least our song's applicable, with love being in the air and all," Sarah added. "Josh and Krystal, Rachel and Eric—"

"What?!" exclaimed Rachel. "I do *not* like Eric—"

"Then why all the dreamy staring and blushing?"

"I was staring at Nathan. Besides, you know I can't stand Eric…"

"Hmm…" Sarah narrowed her eyes quite uncertainly.

"Oh, fine." Rachel wrinkled her nose. "He's not so bad anymore. He's actually sort of sweet. But I wish he wasn't so cute…makes me anxious…"

"Cuter than Nathan?" Sarah grinned, making no effort to conceal the mischievous twinkle in her eye.

"Of course not," Rachel snapped defensively. "But at least he talks to me more than Nathan does—sometimes, at least. Nathan acts so weird other times, like when he was asking me to the ball…"

"I think he just gets nervous around you—" Chasmira began.

"Oh, Nathan's just a dunderhead," Hailey cut her off, ignoring the livid look flashing on Rachel's face. "You should totally go for Eric."

"Oh, no." Rachel shook her head. "I had enough of that when we were younger: Eric crushing on me, driving me crazy…hope that never happens again, even if he *is* cuter and sweeter now…"

"Trust me," Sarah said. "I've seen him looking at another girl already. Besides, you really shouldn't be mean to him just because you don't want him to like you."

"Yeah, you're right," Rachel admitted. "I'll *try* to be nicer."

Chasmira smiled playfully at Sarah. "And *you* shouldn't be mean to Aaron just because he got on your nerves in sixth grade."

Sarah rolled her eyes. "I know, and I'm trying. Have I not been fairly civil?"

"Hmm…*fairly*, I suppose…"

"Speaking of Aaron," said Krystal, "Any clue what he wants to talk to you about this afternoon?"

"Nope."

"He's probably going to ask you out or something," said Rachel.

"Oh, please." Her face flushed scarlet again as she fidgeted. "We're just friends. We're not like that, you should know by now—" and

"'Oh, please' yourself," Sarah snapped. "We all know you like him, and he likes you too."

"Well, we don't really *know* if he likes me." Chasmira squirmed even more ardently.

Sarah rolled her eyes. "For Pete's sake, Anyone who says he likes an apple ten times in one night has to be crazy about you."

"Or maybe he's just crazy." Krystal smirked.

"It was not ten times," Chasmira argued.

"Oh, yes it was," Sarah said. "I counted."

"If you say so. But still, that doesn't mean he likes me. Maybe it was an exceptionally good apple."

They all cast her looks that read *get real*, except Hailey who flashed her a look that clearly stated, *you dunderhead.*

"*Please*," said Rachel. "What about all those e-mails you said he sent you this summer? The phone calls? The inviting you to parties? And he *did* ask you to the ball—"

"As a friend—"

"He either really likes you," Sarah cut in, "or he's just leading you on, and if he's leading you on, well, then, *he's* a fat toad…with warts…with lots of warts…lots of *huge* warts…"

"*Or*," said Chasmira loudly, causing Sarah to snap out of her toad reverie, "maybe he's just being friendly, as usual—"

"Dunderhead!" Hailey exclaimed, unable to contain her annoyance any longer. "Why don't you just tell him you like him? Why can't you just admit the fact that he might like you?"

This question rendered Chasmira speechless and suddenly the wheels in her head started rapidly turning. Why *was* she afraid to admit it? This is what she'd been wanting for years, wasn't it?

"I suppose I've never wanted to get my hopes up," Chasmira explained slowly, trying to understand her own thoughts even as she uttered them. "I mean, I've loved him for so long and I've always told myself that the right guy for me is Aaron, someone very much like him, or no one at all. Yet, I can't just go up and ask him if he likes me, can I? He's the gentleman, and it's his place to ask me. I mean, he at least needs to make the first move. I mean...I know everyone else *says* he likes me, but I want to hear it from him, or at least know it in my heart. I want to be sure he thinks of me as more than just a close friend. I've liked him for so long, and now that there's actually a possibility he might like me in return...I just don't want to give myself false hope. And honestly, I'm fine with our being friends. Always have been. I'd rather him never like me and we be friends forever than to tell him that I like him and things get all weird between us. I've always been content with our friendship as it is, and I will continue to be..."

But for how long? She waited and hoped so long for him to like her as she liked him. But everything would work out for the best, she knew. In the meantime, she must pray that Amiel would help her deal with this matter according to His perfect will. But most of all she would have to pray for patience, because deep down, whether she admitted it fully or not, she wondered about his liking her for some time and was beginning to think upon it more seriously with each passing day.

* * *

Chasmira entered the garden and knew right where to head—the phoenix clearing. As she entered, Aaron turned and smiled at her. Instantly, she scolded herself as she flushed bright red. Such a long time had passed since she blushed this much around him. It seemed to be something that ran in annoying, unpredictable cycles for her. He wore not only his brown sweater but his glasses too, making him look even more adorable than the sweater did already.

"Hey." His half-smirk grew just a little.

"Hey," she returned shyly. "You wanted to talk to me?"

"Yep. I wanted to show you something..."

He led her beneath the phoenix tree, crouched down, and so did Chasmira. Beneath the tree, tiny white blossoms grew. Their leaves had not yet unfurled.

"Moon blossoms..." she breathed.

"Yes. Here, this is for you..."

He presented a beautiful corsage of the tiny white blossoms and she took in her breath.

"It's for the ball. Rachel said you were planning to wear white."

"Thank you." She cupped it gently in her hands. "It's so lovely."

"Yes, quite lovely…" For a moment their eyes met and her heart skipped high, fluttering rapidly.

Then she rose. "Well, I really should go."

"Alright. Well, I'll see you later."

"Alright. Thank you again."

She quickly headed from the garden, quite sure she was smiling huger than huge, huger than she'd smiled in eons, as a hopeful elation flooded her heart. Perhaps Aaron really *did* care for her in that way after all. Maybe, just maybe, the one dream she dreamed more than any other really sustained some slight possibility of dawning true someday…

CHAPTER 9

Monday arrived. Only four days remained until the cruise.

Chasmira was just leaving History class when she nearly bumped into—

"Eric!"

"Chasmira! I'm sorry. I didn't see you."

"That's alright. Hey, shouldn't you be in class?"

"Oh, I don't have another class for an hour." Eric flashed that radiant smile. Chasmira felt her cheeks turn bright red. She was growing extremely agitated at this constant reaction by now. Shouldn't all these hormones have phased out in puberty about five years ago?

"Neither do I. So, where are you going?"

"I go to the gym everyday to play foursquare."

"Foursquare?" Chasmira echoed, smiling. "People still play that even in college?"

"Yeah, it's a good way to take out your stress and relax, actually. And the gym's huge. Have you been there?"

"No, I haven't."

"Then may I escort you, Madame?"

He offered his arm, and smiling, she took it.

As they reached the gym, Eric said, "If I'd known you didn't have class at this time, I would've been inviting you to come with me every day. Well, here we are."

As they entered the gym, Chasmira stared around in wonder. It certainly stretched much huger than the gym at the mansion, three times bigger at least. On one end people played Hoverball. At the other end, a heated game of foursquare ensued. In between the two matches, people bumped volleyballs or played table tennis or ice hockey.

"Aaron told me you loved four square. Shall we?"

Chasmira smiled in reply and hurried over with Eric to get in line.

* * *

Foursquare indeed proved to be quite refreshing and the most fun she experienced between classes in a while. Eric was almost as challenging a foursquare rival as Aaron.

Afterwards, Eric and Chasmira made their way to the dining hall for lunch, quickly locating the table where the others gathered.

As they sat down, Aaron glanced up at them suspiciously, frowning a bit as they entered together. Eric appeared far more cheerful than usual and far too elated in Aaron's opinion. Yet he quickly masked these feelings, scolding himself for being so paranoid.

Presently, Krystal, who had gone off to powder her nose, returned, sitting too perkily in her chair. "Do you guys want to see what I learned in fire club today?"

"If we must," Aaron muttered.

She glared at him, then turned and looked down. Two jets of flame shot from her eyes like lasers, burning two holes in the floor.

Tiff promptly repaired the holes, and Krystal turned to Josh. "That's a warning to you for the next time you think of getting me a prank gift."

Josh proceeded to look very sulky at this. As the others laughed, Aaron's sole focus was upon Eric who smiled at Chasmira with unconcealed admiration. He suddenly wished Krystal would shoot those lasers through Eric's head instead. Quickly shaking the thought aside, feeling both surprised at himself and a bit guilty, he returned to eating his potatoes.

* * *

As Aaron exited History class the next day he nearly ran into—
"Sarah, hey."

"Yeah, sure." She sighed impatiently.

"Have you seen Cassy?"

"Oh, she went to the gym with Eric."

Aaron stared at her, blinking incomprehensibly. "With *who*?"

"Eric, you know, Eric Lindauer—the hot, irritating one? They went there yesterday between classes. I think she said something like she was going to go there every day. Gives her something to do between class. They play four square."

"Oh." He tried to conceal the blunt coldness in his voice, but Sarah eyed him curiously. "Alright then. Thanks, Sarah."

"No problem."

Aaron turned around and started back the way he came. He was paying a visit to the gym.

had
* * *

Rachel, Chasmira, and Josh all teamed up, trying to get Eric out for ten minutes, but Eric proved both too swift and skilled for them. He was the declared champion of four square and wasted no time in showing everyone.

Eric suddenly hit the ball in the left corner and Chasmira dove, just managing to catch it. Two seconds later, he was slamming it in the right corner, and, arms flailing wildly, she missed the ball by a few inches.

Walking off, she cast him an annoyed glare, but he just smiled innocently, nodding his head towards her and calling, "Good game, Madame." She couldn't help but laugh as she joined Krystal watching on the side lines.

"Hey, aren't you going to play?"

"Nope. Might mess up my hair."

Chasmira rolled her eyes. This should've been sadly obvious.

Krystal's head perked with slight interest. "Hey, Aaron just entered."

"Really?" Chasmira's eyes lit up. "Where is he?"

"In line, I believe—"

Chasmira rushed over, stumbling ~~as she rushed towards~~ him.

"Hey, Aaron!"

"Hey, Cassy." He cast his charming half-grin ~~as she approached~~. "Class was cancelled, and I have an hour before my next class, so I figured I would come down here and play a while."

"Eric just got me out."

"Yes, I saw." Aaron's tone grew a bit less friendly, eyes darkening just a tad. He ~~Aaron~~ drew silent, and after standing in awkward quiet a few minutes, Chasmira announced, "I'm gonna use the restroom. I'll be right back."

"Okay."

Chasmira sauntered off to the bathroom, washed her hands, and fixed her hair. Then she fixed it again. And again. Then she snapped back to her senses and realized —liking Aaron was making her paranoid about her hair, just like Krystal. She shuddered. No boy was going to make her *that* crazy.

Chasmira decided her hair looked fine, and if Aaron really liked her, he wouldn't care what her hair looked like. She never worried about such things before. Still, as she exited the bathroom, she couldn't help but continue to wonder why he was acting so unnervingly strange as of late...

As Chasmira approached the gym, a loud commotion echoed from within, people shouting and cheering more explosively than usual. *What in the world is going on?* She furrowed her brow in confusion, quickening her pace.

Upon entering, she noticed everyone gathered around the foursquare arena. It seemed everyone in the gym dropped what they were doing just to watch. Quickly locating Krystal, she rushed to stand beside her.

"What's going—?" She stopped abruptly as she caught a glimpse of the madness unfurling before her.

Aaron was already in second square and hotly competing with Eric for first. The two boys batted the ball back and forth with such an intense fury that the ball seemed to rumble with a sonic boom with each strike they took. Chasmira could not see Eric's face, but Aaron's brow furrowed in determination. His eyes flashed fierce and alert, watching Eric's every sly move, returning with plenty of his own. If Chasmira didn't know better, she would've thought she could detect a glimmer of something like anger in Aaron's eye.

"Wow," Krystal breathed, "We should get them together more often. I've never seen such a heated game..."

Everyone stood enthralled in the game, even Josh and Jarrett, the other two players in the arena. All seemed anxious to see who would triumph and how.

Suddenly, Eric slammed the ball hard in the corner of Aaron's square. The ball soared high in the air, and Aaron tried to fly up to get it, but all he could muster was a short hover. The ball plummeted back down, bouncing in Aaron's square a second time.

Eric cheered loudly, and the gym erupted with applause.

Aaron slammed the ball at Eric before storming off, scowling. His face glowed red and stormy with embarrassment. It wasn't bad enough he lost to Eric, that half the school saw it and joined in the triumphant chorus. Chasmira cheered too. He saw her.

"Hey, Aaron, where are you going?" she asked as he walked past.

"I have class," he muttered sharply, hurrying from the gym.

"I thought he didn't have class for an hour." Chasmira frowned, staring after him perplexed. *you*

Krystal shrugged. "Guys are weird. Come on. Let's get in line so we can get Josh out."

"What about your hair?"

"Oh, I'd risk even my *hair* to get Josh out." She grinned impishly and, with a small grin, Chasmira followed her at the end of the line.

CHAPTER 10

Sarah glanced up. "So, you ready for the cruise tomorrow?" All the girls gathered in their rooms, finishing packing. Hailey was done already and joined Rachel, Sarah, Krystal, and Chasmira in their room. Rachel sat and jumped on her suitcase, trying desperately to force it closed. The other girls tried to tell her it was a hopeless cause as there was twice as much stuff as there was suitcase, but she remained bound and determined to squish it all in there.

"Yup," Krystal sighed, "Can't wait for that ball."

"Yeah," agreed Sarah. "And I'm sure *some* people are especially looking forward to it." Sarah cast Chasmira a sly smile, but she only frowned.

"Did anyone notice that Aaron was acting odd today? He was a bit...distant at supper. And when he was talking, he was a bit sharp, especially—"

"At Eric?" Sarah suggested, and Chasmira started. "Yes, I noticed. He's jealous."

"Jealous?" Chasmira stared. "What does he have to be jealous of? He knows how much I like him—"

"Does he? He only just asked you to the ball. You've never gone out. For all he knows, you could just have some passing crush on him. I mean, Eric's hot, maybe he thinks that—"

"Oh, no. Eric's got nothing on Aaron. I mean, he's definitely cute, but Aaron is so much cuter—"

"Oh, *please*," Rachel grunted, still trying to squash her suitcase closed. "Eric is the cute one—"

Her suitcase suddenly snapped shut, and they all looked over in surprise, except Hailey who sat with the usual, placid look plastered on her face.

Curious, Rachel reopened it. All her possessions had shrunk.

"Oh, thanks, Hailey. But why didn't you do that sooner?"

Hailey shrugged. "It was fun watching you."

Rachel rolled her eyes. "Figures..."

"Look," Chasmira said. "Eric and I are just friends. Aaron knows that. I'm just being friendly."

"Well, I think Sarah's right," Krystal said. "If you get *too* friendly, you could give both Eric *and* Aaron the wrong idea."

"Yeah, I'd be careful if I were you," Sarah agreed.

"Okay, okay," sighed Chasmira.

After saying their prayers, praying especially for tomorrow's journey, they crawled into bed, dressed warmly in their nightgowns. Krystal wore curlers as well as cucumbers over her eyes which made Sarah mumble, "Well, that's a new one. Hope they're not from Josh or she'll have frogs or something leaping from her eyes in the morning…"

They stifled down a laugh and they slipped beneath the covers.

CHAPTER 11

The morning started off with the intriguing news that Josh was caught sleep-walking throughout the boys' dorms at four in the morning, chanting, "We're going on a cruise today." This caused most of the boys to groan and cast him very nasty glares, but, finally, someone threw a pillow at him to wake him up, after which all the boys proceeded to beat him with pillows.

Of course, the pillow battle caused the boys either to be late to breakfast or to reach the dining common looking rather hap-hazard, shirts on backwards, pants on inside out. Josh himself completely forgot to button his shirt which caused many girls to giggle or squeal but sent Pro. Miner into a rage, threatening five times to kick him off the cruise and at least twice threatening him with bodily harm. Mr. Root, who was in charge of the trip, assured Josh he would be going, but he better not catch him "flashing his chest to the ladies" anymore, as he awkwardly put it.

So by early afternoon, all of last year's high school Celestials boarded the *Coral 3,* a huge. elegant ship.

Mr. Root led the boys to their quarters on one side of the ship while Mrs. Miner led the girls to theirs.

Sarah, Rachel, Chasmira, Hailey, Tiff, and Krystal were grateful to share one of the rooms together. It was spacious, with voluminous beds covered with soft blankets and puffy pillows. The closet was huge which was fortunate as Krystal's things filled half of it. The bathroom too was bright, clean, and sported a whirlpool tub.

"Better get our showers before Krystal does," Rachel muttered to Chasmira. "Or she'll be using all the water with that tub…"

"So now that we're unpacked, what do we do?" asked Sarah.

"Mr. Root said to head down to the ship's dining hall at noon," reminded Hailey. "It's eleven thirty. We should probably go."

Rachel handed Hailey the map of the ship, and after the girls designated her as their leader, Hailey led them downstairs to the grand double doors which led to the of the dining hall. They received orders to wait outside until either Mr. Root or Mrs. Miner arrived.

Presently, the rest of the high school seniors started arriving. Aaron, Josh, Nathan, and Sam arrived lastly, huffing and puffing, appearing quite out of breath.

"What happened to *you* guys?" Krystal asked as everyone stared at them.

"Josh read the map wrong," Nathan said.

"It was upside down." Sam glared at Josh.

"We were worried we'd miss lunch," added Aaron.

Krystal stared at them in disbelief. "Wait. You put *Josh* in charge?"

"Hey, where's Eric?" asked Rachel.

"Oh, he's somewhere," Aaron shrugged.

"How profound..."

"I think he was, erm, 'indisposed' when we left, if you get my meaning," said Josh.

Sarah made a face. "You know, we really didn't need to know that."

"Know what?" Eric suddenly squeezed through the crowds to join them.

Presently, Mr. Root arrived, announcing everyone could head into the dining hall.

The dining hall was as elegant as the rest of the place, with purple cloths on the long tables, a sparkling chandelier overhead, ornate silverware, and fine china with tiny violet blossoms painted on each plate and cup.

After praying and asking Amiel's blessing on the meal, food magically appeared before them and they all dug in.

Rachel loaded her plate with bacon, casting Josh suspicious glances as he stared at her plate. There seemed to be no doubt in her mind that he was concocting some plan to spoil her precious bacon as usual.

Aaron succeeded in insulting Sarah by calling her a pig or a wasp or something of that nature. No one really heard the exact comment for Sam was excitedly and rather loudly commenting on the herbs in his soup. Krystal proceeded to burn Aaron's food, but Josh elbowed her to stop her from doing so and she burned a hole in the floor instead. Tiff quickly repaired it, sighing as if growing weary of following Krystal around and fixing all the damage she caused from her momentary yet still quite damaging temper tantrums.

That afternoon, they were to stay in their quarters the rest of the evening as a special, private party was being held on the ship. Tomorrow they would be free to explore.

"Yet another field trip turned annoying after all," sighed Aaron. "We *are* in college. They could just tell us where the party's at and tell us to keep away..."

Aaron grumbled all the way up the stairs until Krystal blazoned a hole in the step right below his feet. He jumped before glaring in a very unforgiving manner at her and returned more ardently to his grumbling whilst Tiff sighed extremely loudly before patching up the gaping hole.

Aaron, Nathan, Sam, and Eric shared a room, and as they unpacked, Nathan sighed. "Well, tomorrow's the big day of the ball."

"Yep," said Aaron. "And then we arrive on Prismatic."

"And then, after a week, we go back to school," Eric added.

They glared at him as though it was perfectly unacceptable to speak of school during vacation.

38

"Anyways," Nathan said. "I *am* a bit nervous about tomorrow. The ball, I mean. Hope I don't step all over poor Rachel's toes…"

"Well, you can always step all over Lucy's if you get the chance." Eric smirked. "I heard her talking to Anita in the hallway. Plans to 'win you back' from Rachel tomorrow."

Nathan rolled his eyes at this while Aaron turned curiously to Eric. "What about you? Who're you dancing with? Never did get a date, did you?"

"No…" A smile spread across his face. "Chasmira promised me a dance though."

"Oh." Aaron proceeded to shove his shirt into the drawer rather roughly.

"Just one dance, eh?" Nathan said. "No one else?"

"Nope. Just a dance with Chasmira. It was very sweet of her to ask."

Aaron spun around. "What? *She* asked you?"

"Yes, felt sorry for me, I think, about not having a partner and all. Still, it was sweet."

"Yes, that's Chasmira for you," Sam said.

"Yes, indeed," mumbled Aaron, turning back to the drawer and proceeding to smooth out the shirt as he inwardly fumed. It was bad enough Eric started talking about Chasmira almost as much as he did himself lately. It was bad enough he always commented how pretty she was and went off gallivanting with her, playing foursquare and who knew what else right under his nose. But now she was asking him for dances? That seemed too much.

Aaron suddenly felt an urge to throw something very hard or sharp at Eric's head. Then he stopped himself, freezing, trying to gulp great, calming breaths. Why should he feel this way? Surely he wasn't jealous. So what if Eric and Chasmira were friends? So what if they spent time by themselves? So what if Eric was tall, handsome, charming, interesting… Nothing could ever jeopardize his friendship with Chasmira. But what if Eric began to desire more than a friendship..? Besides, it wasn't like he and Chasmira were dating themselves. *I mean, I asked her to the ball, but that isn't really a date and doesn't really mean anything, right?* Chasmira liked Aaron for quite a while, and while he only just began to really like her as more than a friend last year, well, if he hadn't made a move yet, he couldn't expect her to wait forever, could he? Still, none of these thoughts reduced his intense desire to pulverize Eric's head with one of the lamps in their room, lamps that were fast growing very tantalizing…

CHAPTER 12

Everyone arose at six thirty, some more promptly than others, and met in the hallway by the stairs. All of the girls were assembled when the first of the boys, Sam, Nathan, and Aaron, dragged down the hallway, looking more than a little sleepy and thus more than a little irritated.

As Sarah announced how tired she was, Aaron glared viciously at her. "Tired? Sarah, you want to know what tired is? Tired is having Andrew's and Daniel's room right next to yours when they stay up all night giggling."

"Whoa, whoa, wait a sec." Rachel stared at Aaron. "*Giggling*? For one thing, it's kinda wrong for guys to *giggle,* and for another, *all night long*?"

Andrew the Washandzee and Daniel the Forest-footer suddenly walked around the corner, looking bright and fully awake. *presently*

"Well, well, aren't we chipper this morning," mumbled Sam.

Rachel eyed Andrew curiously. "Hey, Andrew. Care to tell us why you were *giggling* last night?"

"Giggling?" Andrew cast her a perplexed look. "All I know is I was sick all last night, throwing up."

Sarah stared at Aaron. "How in the world do you confuse giggling with barfing?"

Nathan shrugged. "Giggling, upchucking—it's all the same at three o'clock in the morning."

Sarah rolled her eyes.

Aaron was just retelling the giggling account and Andrew was defending himself with his upchucking account when Josh strolled around the corner. "Hey, sorry, that was me. I'm on the other side of your room, Aaron. Someone put some kind of giggling jinx into my toothpaste. Wonder who..."

Josh's gaze drifted accusingly to Krystal who promptly blushed, turning away as the other boys cast her rather nasty glares, particularly Aaron, Sam, and Nathan.

Then ~~Suddenly~~, Mr. Root appeared, announcing cheerily, "Alright, folks. Ready for a hearty breakfast and a busy day? Come on, breakfast is in the ballroom today."

As they followed him down the stairs, Aaron mumbled to Krystal, "Why couldn't you have put some sort of jinx in *his* toothpaste?"

Upon entering the ballroom, the girls stared in awe at the grand chandelier, marble floor and pillars, and sprawling staircase that swept in a wide arc on the far side. The boys tried to be amused, but half didn't really care, and the other half would've cared only if the room contained several comfy, sound-proofed beds.

"This is the room where the ball shall be held this evening. It's also where all the rest of your breakfasts shall be served the remainder of the trip..."

Stretched Mr. Root led them to the left side of the spacious room where several long banquet tables ~~stood~~, freshly prepared food already laid out on them.

They all found seats(this took some time to work out as there were those who wanted to get as far away from Josh as possible), and when everyone was settled as comfortably as possible, Mr. Root asked Amiel's blessing on the food then bid them all to "dig in."

After breakfast, everyone decided to ~~explore~~ *tour* the ship, the boys exploring up on the deck, the girls amusing themselves in the various shops below.

Chasmira, Hailey, Sarah, and Rachel all sat around bored as Krystal and Tiff sampled all the lipsticks inside "Ross's Glosses," a task they'd been thoroughly accomplishing for a half hour.

As Rachel yawned widely and Hailey irritably mumbled something about wanting to visit the herb store, Sarah chirped, "So, everyone ready for the ball tonight?"

"I don't think I am," Chasmira admitted, and they all looked at her curiously. "I mean, I've hardly ever danced, and it's been ages since I have. I know Aaron can dance, and I don't fancy making a fool of myself in front of him."

Rachel shrugged. "I'm not the greatest either. Or I'd show you."

"I don't plan to dance much," said Sarah.

"Me neither," sniffed Hailey. "I find it such a bore..."

"Oh, I don't find it a bore. I just...er...have other plans for the evening..."

By the smirk and mischievous twinkle in her eye, Chasmira felt sure those plans involved just that—mischief, and somehow felt that mischief would involve shape-shifting. She'd known Sarah long enough to understand how her impish mind worked.

"Eric!" Rachel suddenly exclaimed, and they all began looking around for him.

"No, he's not *here*." Rachel rolled her eyes. "You think any of the guys would be caught dead in a lipstick store? I meant that he's an excellent dancer. At least, he was two years ago. You should go talk to him. Maybe he'll give you some tips."

"Alright, but when? We don't have all that much time before we have to get ready for the ball."

"Oh, go ahead," drawled Hailey. "We'll wait here for Krystal and Tiff. Besides, by the looks of things, it doesn't seem as though we're going to make it to the herb store."

Chasmira did not possess the heart to tell her that she did not exactly find this news disappointing. So after promising she would see them in a couple hours, she departed Ross's Glosses, grateful for a valid excuse to leave.

* * *

The lip gloss escapade finally finished, the girls sat in their room, dreamily discussing the ball and their dates—all save Hailey who huddled in a corner, mumbling stormily about the injustices of herb deprivation...

"So...who are you going with, Tiff?" Krystal asked, trying to conceal her intense curiosity, but if it didn't reflect heavily in her voice, it dripped from the longing gaze she cast her friend.

Unabashed, Tiffany beamed, clutching the dress close to her heart, declaring, "It's a secret. I can't tell you."

She giggled, twirling, eyes dancing with child-like excitement.

"Now, if you'll excuse me..."

As she bustled from the room, leaving the girls to stare wondering after her, Krystal heaved a deep sigh, crying anxiously, "Ooo, who could it be?"

"Caleb? Antoine? Josh?"

Krystal rolled her eyes at Rachel. "No, all losers, her tastes are more refined. Besides, Josh is *my* date."

"You'd really put it past that dunderhead to take two dates to the dance?" Hailey inquired, eyes flashing unconcealed sarcasm.

"What about Jarrett?" suggested Chasmira. "She's been tutoring him in English a lot lately."

Krystal snorted. "Jarrett gets some girl to tutor him for *every* class, hopeless soul, still too busy ogling at them to make decent grades. No, Jarrett might be a cover, but nothing more. Not her type."

"But do we even *know* her type?" asked Rachel. "Has she even seen a boy the whole time she's gone to school with us?"

Krystal opened her mouth to retort but then closed it as her brows slowly knit confusedly together.

As Chasmira thought, she too frowned. Many flirters and wanna-bes pursued Tiff over the years, but she did nothing beyond flirt back, at least so far as she knew. Was she just shy, withdrawn, not wanting everyone prying into her business? Or was she afraid they might not approve? Despite her own taste in men, Krystal was very opinionated when it came to her friends' choices in dates, and she was supposed to be Tiffany's best friend, after all...

"Well, if she's been able to hide it this far..." Rachel muttered.

"Guess we'll just have to wait and see," Chasmira finished for her.

* * *

Tiffany knocked anxiously on his door, waited an impatient half second, then rapped fervently again.

"Just a minute, just a minute, honestly," he growled from within, and she beamed. The mere sound of his voice thrilled her, its fluidity luxurious even when irritated.

As he threw the door open, his eyes flashed stormily, but upon seeing her, they lightened with surprise, and while he did not smile, he stood aside, arm floating like a graceful cloud as he motioned her in, saying quietly, "Come in, Tiffany."

Bustling in, she cast a quick glance about the room—singular bed, curtains pulled shut tight, several flashlights dancing strange orange circles upon the walls and the books scattered about the room. She shook her head. "Honestly, when are you going to stop brooding in lonely, dark apartments? If you're trying to remain inconspicuous, stepping out into fresh air or socializing a bit might be the safer route."

"I'll go outside when my mere nature doesn't make me a freak in doing so," he snarled, his dark gaze staring absently at the far wall, "and I'll socialize when there's a purpose in doing so, when I can get close to people without ruining both them and myself..."

"Cheery today, aren't we?" Bouncing off the bed, she twirled about, the white ruffles of the dress' hem swirling in a wide arc, glittering a mysterious orange-white, like a candle's flame, in the strange glow of the room.

"Isn't it exquisite? I thought we could do a classic black-and-white theme, don't you think? Everyone's into color this year, but I—"

"What are you talking about, Tiffany?" he snapped, eyes flashing coldly at her.

She shuddered, smile faltering a bit though she continued confidently, "Look, I know you hate social affairs, but you don't even have to ask me out. I'm asking you. I mean, I know we haven't talked since last semester, I know things have been tough. I miss you too, but that's why I think we should take this opportunity to do something together—"

"I don't accept," he said bluntly, flatly.

She stared, blinking. "What?"

"You said you were asking me. Well, I don't accept."

Staring harder, she blinked faster, fighting back the coming tears. Surely she heard him wrong, surely...

But as ever, if she doubted his words, his eyes communicated his message more fervently, leaving no room for doubt.

Dropping her voice to a whisper, all strength suddenly robbed from her by the hateful tears, she sank to the edge of the bed, whispering, "Dristann, what is it? Why do you keep avoiding me? I know you think I don't see you when I pass you in the halls, but I do. You can't hide from me. Don't you know how it hurts for you to look straight at me as if I were less than air? Don't you care, does nothing bother you anymore? Have I done something wrong, are you ashamed of me..?"

She always wanted to be strong for him because he needed that, but now her voice cracked and she looked away as the fresh tears torrented down her cheeks. She'd allowed herself to feel, risking the loss of that strong, tight barrier. Now, her vulnerable heart attacked, she couldn't just think of him, she couldn't stop the overwhelming flood of sadness, pain, anger, betrayal...

"No," he said, still coldly, but as she looked up, he did not stare at her but at the floor. "No," his voice but a small hum, "I feel no shame in anyone—but myself."

As his eyes flashed sharply up to meet hers, powerful waves of coldness, bitterness undulating within them, he snarled, "You think I don't see how you hurt? That I don't care? That's the one thing that hurts me, the one thing still capable of making me feel hurt, keeping me human—your hurt, Tiffany. Your hurt hurts me."

"Then why don't you act like it?" she breathed, her chest constricting as if that hard gaze alone made it a struggle to breathe. "Last semester, at the wedding, when you held my hand...and now you don't even touch me with your eyes...you can't understand how empty...you used to look at me like I was the most beautiful thing in the world..."

He chewed his lip frantically, the deep mixture of emotions swelling in his eyes intensifying, his body shaking until at last, in one, graceful stride, he sat beside her, whispering in her ear, "You are the most important thing in *my* world, in *our* world. That's all that matters. And you are the most beautiful thing in this or any other world."

As his breath tickled her ear, cool and sweet-scented, sending delighted shudders rippling from her face down to her toes, he took her hand, squeezing it. Her eyes shut. Ecstasy pumped through her as he traced the skin of her hand ever so lightly, as he continued to breathe softly, steadily upon her cheek, intoxicating her with favorite smells, ensnaring her mind until there was only him. She drank in his breath, his touch, his very presence beside her as if they were more vital, more satisfying, more needful than the very oxygen of that same air. As he brushed away the tears, making her forget what tears were, what the need for them was, all definition of sorrow, pain, regret, shame fleeing from her mind as she readily let him hold it captive, he whispered, "Will you attend the ball with me, Miss Tiffany?"

"Yes," she breathed, shuddering as the fingers wiping away the tears trailed ever so softly, like a lilting laughter, down her neck to rest on her shoulder. She smiled as he began to massage her favorite spot, slowly, eeking out the pleasurable pain.

"The time draws close, you know," he said. "My aunt...if she is not successful in her mission, she will choose me. She will make me, you know this..."

"You don't have to," she whispered, rolling her head slowly as he worked his fingers deeper into her back.

"But I already have...you know what will happen at the ball tonight...but I refuse to do anything else for now. I won't help you, nor will I help her. Funny, you'd think one of my kind would be able to hold more influence on your weak kind..."

"But you do," she breathed, opening her eyes at last, gazing up at him hazily. The orange light danced a strange sort of halo upon his snow-golden hair, as if he were a sprite wearing a crown of fire, entrapping her both against her will and yet not all at once. He lifted her chin ever so gently so that her lips just barely missed brushing his, and as she breathed him in once more, the heavy scent ensnaring all reason, all other thoughts but that of lunging herself into his arms—

He released her, and jerking out of her daze abruptly, she sat stunned, a bit dizzy. Yet even as her vision cleared, she gazed up at him in awe, hope and doubt mingling in her eyes as she whispered hesitantly, "Do...are you sure you really want to go with me?"

"Yes," the single word pleading with all the sincerity in the world, even as did his torment-stricken eyes. "How I try to detach myself from everything so that when the time comes, I can detach myself even from *it*...but you...*you* keep me human, remind me who I am. I just can't seem to stop feeling with you. I just can't seem to hurt you. It hurts too much..."

"Why do you think I always chose you?" she whispered. "Because I saw what you could be. I saw what others might not see, and I wanted to save that part of you, make it grow...no matter how painful that has become for me..."

He sighed deeply, as if releasing years of torture in that one, heavy breath. "I wish you chose another. I wish I bore the strength to refrain from hurting you over and over..."

"But that's what good friends do," she said tenderly, "they keep coming back, keep hoping, praying, keep worrying when their friend strays from the path of the light. I only want what's best for you, Dristann, I love you—"

She gasped, fear flooding her eyes as if she uttered a forbidden curse.

"What?" he breathed, confused hurt flickering in his eyes.

"I've felt it a long time, meaning it," she said quietly, "but I know it's hard for you to express emotions, I know it's uncomfortable when others—I've just been putting it off, not wanting to scare you."

"It's not so hard with you," he assured. "But while I care deeply, I'm not ready to return the words. It's hard sometimes to know whether I truly love you, though I want to, or whether I just need you...but I can't tell you how much it means to hear those words for the first time."

She stared at him incredulously. "Not even..."

"Does my mother seem like the kind interested in demonstrating true love?" he mumured. "I know you know her story well too."

"I'm so sorry," she breathed, trembling as she dared to caress his cheek with the palm of her hand.

"Don't be sorry." He touched her own cheek. "Only love me..."

* * *

After roaming the decks for fifteen minutes, Chasmira ran into Jarrett who announced that Nathan, Eric, and Aaron had gone back to their room. He gave her their room number and she continued her search, uncertain if she was allowed on the guys' floor. Then again, the guys were given permission to come to the girls' floor to pick them up for the night's "date," and no one exactly forbid her to go up there.

Chasmira arrived and rapped lightly on the door. Within, she heard footsteps, someone tripping on something and yelling, "Ouch! Dad-gum Cheetos..." Then the door opened and Aaron's face lit up.

"Oh, hey, Cassy. Come on in."

"Actually, I was hoping to talk to Eric."

"Oh, sure, he's here, come on in—"

"Alone, please."

Aaron's smile suddenly vanished. He forced himself not to look concerned or disturbed by this, which only resulted in him blinking very rapidly, his eyebrows wrinkled as he smiled a contorted half-grin.

"Oh, uhh...yeah. Umm, Eric, door."

Aaron sauntered back into the room, leaving Chasmira to wonder about his strange reaction, but then Eric bounced into view, cheerful as always. "Oh, hey, Cassy—" Aaron shot Eric a sharp look—"How's it going?"

"Fine...umm...could I talk to you for a second?"

"Sure."

Eric stepped from the room and closed the door. He and Chasmira walked down the hall a little ways before she stopped to face him.

"Look," she said quietly. "I need to ask you a favor."

"Anything." His heart leapt as he gazed into those deep, blue eyes.

"You know the ball tonight?"

"Yeah."

"Rachel told me...Well, I haven't danced in so long...I was wondering if I could practice with you so I don't make an idiot of myself tonight. Rachel said you were quite good."

Eric flashed those brilliant, blush-worthy, white teeth, eyes dancing. "Sure. No problem. When do you want to start?"

"Well, we don't have much time. How about I meet you in the café in an hour?"

"Okay. No problem."

"Thanks." Chasmira beamed. "Well, see ya later."

Eric watched Chasmira walk off down the hall then turned and headed back to his room.

"What did Chasmira want?" Aaron asked immediately.

"Oh, nothing." Eric shrugged, grinning as he exited into the bathroom.

The urge to throw something at Eric's head promptly returned to Aaron.

* * *

"Where are you going?" asked Nathan as Eric prepared to leave. Aaron sat on the bed, eying him suspiciously.

"Oh, I'm meeting someone downstairs," said Eric nonchalantly, shrugging.

"Who? Chasmira?" Aaron sneered.

"Uhh...yes, actually."

"Then I'll come with you." Aaron jumped off the bed.

"Look, I don't think Chasmira would like that—"

"How would you know what she would like? You've only known her a few weeks—"

"Look, I don't know what you're problem is lately—"

"My problem?!" Aaron echoed, his voice rising, cheeks flashing an unhealthy scarlet. "You're constantly hitting on the girl I like and you wonder what my problem is?!"

Eric suddenly grew very pale.

"You and Chasmira...you like Chasmira..?"

"You always were a little slow when it came to social skills," Aaron sneered. "Yes, I like Chasmira, and she likes me."

"Look, Aaron. I had no clue—"

"No clue?! How could you not have a clue?! I asked her to the dance, didn't I?!"

"Yes, but I assumed...I thought you were going as friends. I see now how foolish—look, I'm sorry—"

"I suppose you're still going to meet her though?" Aaron hissed coolly, glaring with a fiery gaze. Eric felt rotten, but how could he break his word to Chasmira, especially since he realized now she asked him to come on Aaron's account?

"Yes. I told her I would—"

Aaron shook his head and hurried to the bathroom, slamming the door. "Why don't you just tell her you'll be taking her to the dance as well?!"

"Aaron—"

Eric sighed. He then glanced at Nathan who merely shrugged his shoulders, and Eric knew there was nothing more he could do until Aaron had sufficient time to cool off. So off he scurried to the café.

CHAPTER 13

The girls' quarters was sheer madness. Girls raced around in robes and curlers. A few ran about in flip-flops, including Rachel who stumbled over her over-sized, horse-shaped slippers, hissing as her curlers tousled on top of her head and in front of her eyes, blinding her momentarily.

The halls and rooms bustled with cataclysmic activity as the myriad of girls prepared for the ball, arranging makeup, making final adjustments to dresses with loose buttons, asserting that gloves and jewelry matched perfectly.

Only a half hour remained until the ball and still Krystal hogged the bathroom. The other girls need only get dressed, complete half-started hair and make-up, but with four of them, that didn't leave much time. Rachel and Hailey already abandoned hope, traversing the hall to borrow another of the girl's bathrooms. Chasmira and Sarah sat on the edge of the bed, casting skeptical looks at each other that declared they were about ready to do the same when Krystal finally emerged in her soft, purple, sleeveless, glittering gown trailing the floor. Her curls were piled neatly on top of her head and purple dragonfly clips sparkled in her hair.

"You look great." Sarah smiled, hurrying with her periwinkle, long-sleeved, off-the-shoulders gown into the bathroom. "Mmm...smell great too..."

Krystal beamed. "It's Midnight Passion, the new perfume Josh got me."

Sarah paused at this bit of news to cast Chasmira a concerned glance before entering the bathroom, and Chasmira nearly laughed.

"Well, I'm going to sit down and read until we go." Krystal snatched up the book lying on her bed. "I'm almost finished—"

Suddenly her eyelids grew heavy, then closed, and she collapsed on the bed.

Chasmira stared in shock, then got up and slowly headed over to Krystal. Was she okay? She bent low, listening carefully. Yes, Krystal's breathing was steady, and very calm, almost like she slept. Suddenly, it struck Chasmira, and she leaned closer, sniffing at Krystal's perfume. For a moment, her eyelids grew heavy and she reeled, then stumbled back, dizzy a moment. The perfume was really a sleeping potion.

Sarah promptly emerged, looking gorgeous in her periwinkle, and cast one, short glance at Krystal. "The perfume?"

"Think so."

"Figures. She gave him some cologne to make him go to sleep so he'd miss the ball and wouldn't be gawking at me all night. Besides, she's fed up with him anyways, said she'd rather find someone else to dance with. Though I wonder why Josh sent *her* some of the stuff...a bit annoying, her wasting all our bathroom time just so she can look pretty while she snores all night...oh, well, bathroom's ready. Best hurry. Aaron will be here soon..."

Her eyes sparkled playfully at Chasmira who smiled, blushing as she slipped into the bathroom.

When the two girls were ready, they made sure Krystal was comfortable on the bed. Then Sarah bid Chasmira good-bye and good luck, announcing she would see her at the ball as Chasmira sat on the edge of the bed, waiting patiently.

She waited. And she waited. Six o'clock came, five after passed. Chasmira frowned. It wasn't at all like Aaron to be late. Rather, he was usually annoyingly early. Perhaps he wasn't feeling well? Perhaps she better go and find out. And so, after checking upon Krystal one last time and finding her snoring deeply, she exited the room.

The hall bustled with couples, both those from the school as well as other passengers on the ship. As she headed to the boys' quarters, she spotted Rachel and Nathan, arms linked, Rachel smiling in an elated sort of way. They passed Lucy who walked loosely arm in arm with Jarrett Slater until Nathan and Rachel slipped by and she scowled, drawing Jarrett's arm painfully close to her. He yelped, glaring. Chasmira thought she heard Lucy mutter something like, "I'll get you, my Naty-poo..."

Finally finding herself before the boys' door, she knocked.

Eric answered and for a moment stood utterly stunned, and Chasmira took the chance to stare too. He seemed twice as handsome as usual in his raven black tuxedo.

She quickly snapped back into reality. "Is Aaron okay? He didn't show up."

"Uhh, dunno, he's still in the bathroom. I'll go see," Eric muttered quickly in a sort of uncomfortable tone, an awkward smile upon his face.

For a moment, silence ensued, but then a voice stirred within—it was Aaron's.

"I told you I'm not going—you take her—"

"Aaron, you can't not go at all, she's been looking so forward to it—"

This was followed by a more hushed, though equally intense-sounding conversation, none of which Chasmira heard, yet she heard enough for her heart to begin to sink. Why didn't Aaron want to take her? He sounded angry. But why? What had she possibly done?

Eric presently opened the door and smiled more than a bit awkwardly, "Uhh...he's just running behind. He'll meet you there."

"Thanks." She offered a smile in an attempt to conceal the fact that she overheard any of the conversation. Yet as soon as she turned and started towards the ballroom, a tear slid down her cheek. She quickly tried to blink back the entourage of hateful tears. She was not going to let Aaron spoil her night, even if part of it being her night was that it was supposed to be *their* night. She would find Aaron later and figure out what was bothering him, straighten things out. In the mean while, she would enjoy herself at the ball as best she could.

* * *

Aaron entered the ballroom. It was teaming with activity and bright colors as couples danced. The scents of delicious foods wafted up from the tables lining the walls. But none of this held any sway upon Aaron. It all seemed distant, insignificant to him. He noticed it, and yet, he did not really see any of it. His single thought, his only reality in that moment, was Chasmira. He knew he messed things up, acting like a total idiot. Even if Chasmira *did* like Eric, well, he promised to take her to the ball. What kind of friend just abandoned her, screwing up what was supposed to be a fun night for her? He took a deep breath and slowly descended the grand, winding stairs that led down into the ballroom.

He scanned the room but located no sign of Chasmira. Instead, he found himself running into Eric.

"Oh, hey," said Aaron stiffly. "Chasmira here?"

"Yeah, I think she was looking for you."

"Where is she?"

"Oh, somewhere. I was just getting her some punch."

Aaron suddenly felt like punching Eric, but he tried to shake this now common thought aside. He succeeded in this, but his thoughts were interrupted by Hailey calling, "Hey, Aaron!"

Presently, Hailey arrived in a rainbow-colored gown, followed by Rachel who sported navy blue, as well as Nathan and Sam in their black tuxes matching Aaron's.

"So, where's Chasmira?" asked Sam.

"Oh, somewhere," Aaron said quickly. Sam was one person oblivious to any of the goings on between him, Eric, and Chasmira, and he wished to keep it that way.

Suddenly, he noticed, "Hey, where's Sarah and Krystal?"

Hailey shrugged. "Oh, Sarah was off impersonating Krystal last I saw. Something about she didn't want Josh following her around and staring at her all night, which of course could really be an insult towards Krystal when you think about it..."

Sam nodded. "But then I told her about Josh falling asleep and she sighed relief, then changed into some other person."

Before Aaron could ask what happened to Josh or Krystal, Rachel added, "And Krystal won't be coming. Sarah said Josh put some kind of sleeping draft in her perfume."

"*No way!*" exclaimed Nathan. "We think she did the same thing with his cologne."

48

Aaron sighed, smirking wryly. "Ahh...I always knew they were perfect for each other..."

"Hey, Nathan," Sam elbowed him. "Wanna get some *hors d'oeuvre*?"

Nathan glanced at Rachel.

"Sure, go ahead. I'll get myself some cream puffs later."

"Didn't you want to dance though?"

"We can dance later. I can dance with Aaron for now."

Aaron opened his mouth to protest, but Rachel already swept him onto the dance floor.

"So, cream puffs?" he mused as they mixed in with all the other couples.

"Yep, I've been looking forward to those all night..."

After that, no more conversation ensued. In fact, Aaron's mind wandered anywhere but on the dance floor with Rachel. He constantly strained his neck, looking around her, always searching for *her*...

As they danced, Rachel frowned. "Umm...are you okay?"

"Yeah..." He half-ignored her. "Just looking for Chasmira..."

"Flaming grasshoppers, look at that!"

Aaron whirled, nearly tripping, hoping Rachel's bizarre exclamation revolved around a sighting of Chasmira. Instead, he gazed upon something else stunningly beautiful, if strange and confusing.

A couple graced the topmost step, the young man gazing out calmly yet confidently, the young lady's head raised just a bit, neither too proudly nor too shyly, her eyes sparkling as she glanced at her partner. It was Tiffany, her arm linked in Dristann Malloy's.

As hushed, disbelieving whispers rippled through the room, some approving, others disapproving, all awing whether in wonder or jealousy, the couple descended, a flush just visible as it crept into Tiffany's dark brown cheeks.

The simplicity of their beauty stunned. His snowy skin against his black suit, her dark skin contrasted with the flowing, white ruffles of the strapless dress, they descended like alternating black and white diamonds or like soft ocean foam against harsh, stormy waves. Skin, hair, eyes, dress all glittering, outshining the magnificence of the chandeliers' many crystals.

Suddenly, betwixt the weaving couples, Aaron saw her, and everything else, the music, the waltzing couples, the otherworldly couple drawing all's attention, even the steps on which she stood, faded away. Again, there was only *her* standing out, *she*, his only reality. She just descended the elegant winding stair and stood with such grace and beauty that she reminded him of a princess. Her hair swept up in a shower of curls, and her off-the shoulders dress flowed long, pure white, and glittering. She wore white gloves, dazzling crystal chandelier earrings, and a crystal necklace. The moon blossom corsage lighted upon her wrist as well.

Aaron kept craning his neck to catch a glimpse of Chasmira as he and Rachel twirled. Suddenly she stood beside Eric, talking, laughing, too thoroughly enjoying herself without him...

He stomped hard on the ground.

"Ouch! That's my foot, you idiot!"

As they swirled, ~~Aaron~~ Chasmira suddenly stood alone, and without realizing, he released Rachel, and she crashed to the ground, crying, "Oh, not my ankle!"

Chasmira hummed the tune the violinists played when a voice asked behind her, "May I have this dance?"

"Back already, Eric?"

As she turned though, a fuming Aaron paused but for one, frustrated moment before storming off.

"Aaron?"

While Chasmira raced after Aaron, Rachel still slouched on the ground, rubbing her throbbing ankle.

"Are you okay?"

A grin spread broadly across her lips as she gazed up at Nathan. She grasped his hand ~~as he extended it, helping her up.~~ *extended* *and he helped her up.*

"Do you wanna dance?"

"Sure." The pain in her ankle seemed to miraculously disappear—or at least enough for her to ignore it for a dance with Nathan.

As Rachel and Nathan waltzed across the floor amidst the other happy couples, she couldn't feel greater elation, but after a few moments, she noticed Nathan seemed distracted. He continously strained his neck to see around her. He wasn't watching where he was going and kept stepping all over her feet. She sighed. This reaction felt bad enough coming from Aaron, but must she tolerate it in Nathan as well?

Rachel tried to be patient, but considering she was not generally a patient person, plus the fact that her feet already throbbed from Aaron trampling them and throwing her to the floor, all patience quickly fled.

"Jikes! That's the fifth time you've stepped on my foot! What's the deal with you?"

"Oh, sorry. I'm looking for Lucy."

"For *who*?"

"For Lucy—I'm supposed to dance with her, but—"

"Ugh! What is with you guys tonight?!" She threw her arms up in frustration before storming off in the direction of creampuffs.

"Rachel, wait—it's not like that—"

"Naty, oh my Naty-poo, care for a dance?"

Lucy presently swept a defenseless Nathan off his feet, and soon they ~~entwined~~ *themselves* lost amongst the coiling throng of winding couples.

Sarah meanwhile had loads of fun shape-shifting. She switched between impersonating Josh and Krystal, dancing with lots of cute guys in Krystal form (she figured that Josh deserved to be the jealous one for a change when all those cute guys came calling for Krystal in the days to come), and pulling pranks on other people as Josh. She already made a half dozen girls hiss threats against Josh's life if they ever saw him again, so she decided to play it cool and go about as herself for a while. As she slipped onto the deck to get some fresh air, she noticed Rachel standing and leaning against the railing, popping cream puffs into her mouth at a furious rate, gulping them whole with hardly a chew. Judging by her bulging purse, she stuffed the little handbag with a good two dozen. An overly displeased, infuriated look flashed upon her face as she stared into the ballroom with a death glare, suddenly squeezing one of the cream puffs so hard that its contents splattered all over her dress.

"Snapperdoodle!"

Sarah felt unsure whether it was safe to sidle over and talk to Rachel but decided she would take her chance. After all, Rachel was her best friend's friend, and any friend of Cassy's was a friend of hers. *Well, maybe except for Aaron, but that is beside the point right now.* Sarah was always willing to help a friend in need, so she cautiously approached Rachel. "Umm...are you okay?"

Rachel glanced up. "Oh, hey, Sarah." She proceeded to rub the cream puff contents off of her dress with a napkin, which shredded miserably. Throwing it irritably to the ground, she popped another cream puff in her mouth, muttering, "Yeah, I'm fine."

"You were shoving cream puffs in your mouth like a crazy person, squeezing them like you wanted to pop someone's head off. That's not an 'I'm fine' sign."

"Well...for one thing, I was sorta gorging since my grandma wants me to go on a diet."

A pause ensued in which Sarah skeptically glanced up and down Rachel's slim form. "Is your grandma blind?"

Rachel smiled slightly. "No, just a bit annoying. Says I eat too much."

"Is she the one who sent you the cross-stitch project you've been working on this whole trip?"

"The one I probably won't finish until I'm out of college? Yep, that's her."

Another pause. Rachel still looked mad about something, but behind the mask of anger, hurt and frustration shone in her eyes.

"There's another reason behind your cream-puff binge," Sarah observed.

Rachel's gaze remained locked upon the ballroom. "Well, *look* at those two. This is their second dance." Her eyes flared before softening defeatedly. She sighed.

Sarah gazed in the direction Rachel did, understood, and couldn't resist bursting out laughing.

Rachel stared at her menacingly. "Oh, I see absolutely <u>nothing</u> funny—"

"I'm sorry," Sarah chuckled, unsuccessfully trying to contain herself. "It's just— Nathan and Lucy—if you're worried about them, you have *nothing* to worry about. I've *seen* Nathan in there, and he's *miserable.*"

"If he's so miserable, then why was he looking for her when he was dancing with me?" Rachel snapped, still not seeing the humor in any of this.

Sarah somewhat calmed herself. "I was sneaking around Lucy's room. You see, I turned into her hairbrush, and I tell you she uses some strongly scented shampoo. I nearly gagged. As it is, the smell's enough to make Nathan sufficiently unhappy. Anyhow, I overheard her telling Anyta and Emma that Nathan was going to save her a dance, during which she would 'break the spell that horrid Rachel cast on her Natypoo.' So if I were you, I'd be going in there, 'casting a few spells,' and saving poor Nathan."

Rachel laughed, smiling sincerely. "Thanks. Now that I think about it, I guess I was kinda stupid to think Nathan would fall for Lucy."

"'That's the danger of jealousy,' or whatever wise stuff Chasmira would say in such a situation."

"Yep. Well, you're right. I'm gonna go help Nathan out." As she slipped back into the ballroom, Sarah could hear her scolding herself: "Lucy, of all people! I am such an idiot!"

Sarah sighed contentedly. "And *I* don't like any boy and don't have to worry about the stress of it all. What bliss!" Her eyes narrowed as a mischievous glint entered them. "Hmm...I wonder who I can torture as Caleb..."

While Sarah and Rachel engaged in their discussion on the left side of the deck, Aaron stormed onto the right side, Chasmira rushing to keep up with him, tripping on her long skirt, scolding the dress as she went.

"Aaron, wait!" she called. "Oh, confound these heals!"

Removing the shoes, she raced to catch up with him.

"Aaron, *stop*!" Never was he in such a foul mood, and for a moment it looked like he might not stop but instead fling himself over the railing into the ocean. But he did halt though he did not turn to look at her.

"Aaron, what's *wrong* with you? I've never seen you like this. You ask me to dance, then you vanish...you've been acting like an idiot lately—"

"Well, if I'm such an *idiot*, why don't you just go dance with your boyfriend, Sir Lindauer..."

"My—*Aaron Phillip Ruiz*!" He cringed upon hearing her voice shout his entire name. "Do you *honestly* think—do you *think* Eric and I—why on Earth—?"

"Why wouldn't I?" Aaron snapped, finally wheeling to face her, eyes ablaze. "You two having secret conversations—"

"As if *we* never had—"

"—the way you blush when he compliments you—"

"Oh, *please*, I do that with every boy, even Josh—"

"—dancing with him instead of me—"

"Instead of—oh, no. Wait a sec. You're *jealous*, aren't you?"

"I am not!" he strongly protested, though Chasmira's skeptical eyes flashed with a sheer, unconvinced light.

"You are *too*. Well, I'll have you know that you're *highly* mistaken. I asked Eric to teach me about waltzing so I could surprise you tonight, so I wouldn't make a complete, blundering moron out of myself in front of you. I promised to give him a dance in return. And why would you care anyhow if I liked Eric? What business is it of yours?"

"Because I like you!" he shouted. An awkward silence lingered in which Chasmira could only stare at him in shock, and he suddenly felt a great desire to hide in the nearby pot plant. He didn't exactly plan to tell her quite this way.

But Suddenly though, she smiled shyly yet radiantly, asking quietly, "You do?"

"Yeah, I do," he muttered.

"So...you *were* really jealous?" Chasmira smirked, eyes gleaming slyly.

"Yeah," he admitted. "I guess I kinda was. Don't know what came over me. I feel kinda stupid now. Do you forgive me?"

"Of course, but...why didn't you just tell me you liked me before? You know I've liked you for ages." She glanced away shyly.

Aaron sighed deeply, studying the stars. "Because I didn't want to screw things up."

She glanced up at him curiously, searchingly.

"Chasmira, in the time that we went to different schools...things happened. I've been in some bad relationships in the past, relationships that ended with me no longer being friends with the girls I went out with. So I wanted to tell you how I felt really badly, yet..."

"Yet you were afraid if we got together that would screw up our friendship," Chasmira finished for him quietly.

"Yes." He avoided those bright, understanding eyes. "I wasn't really sure if I was emotionally capable of having a relationship. I'm not sure now. But I thought that if I told you I liked you, then told you that I might not be ready for a relationship, you might get mad, disappointed, that..."

"That I might not want to wait?" she suggested gently. He did not reply, but she could read the answer in his face which pointed towards the deck's floor. His dark eyes held glimmers of emotional torture, undulating like back, painfully stormy waves.

"Aaron," she said in a voice low, firm, yet soft and tender all at once. "I've always appreciated your honesty. It's one of the many things I admire in you. All you would've had to tell me is that you care about me but just want to get to know me better as a friend before we start anything more serious. I would've waited. I've waited for over six years now, haven't I? And I tell you truthfully that I would wait til the end of the world. I've never cared about anyone as I care about you, Aaron, and I don't think I ever could..."

Aaron looked up and saw those gentle sapphires sparkling sincerely. She smiled a small, timid smile, her cheeks flushing a bright red though she spoke confidently.

"So...we can take things slowly?"

"As slow as you want."

They smiled at each other for one slow, invaluable moment. Then Aaron said, "So...you still want to dance?"

"Sure."

They waltzed slowly about the deck for a while then stopped, leaning against the railing and staring into the night sky. Thousands of stars twinkled like tiny diamonds above them.

Chasmira sighed. "It's such a peaceful night."

Suddenly, the moon peeped out from behind the clouds, and as its milky light touched the corsage, the petals of the flowers opened, sparkling brightly.

Chasmira beamed at Aaron, and as his heart pounded against his chest as if trying to leap to embrace her, he returned his half-grin.

Suddenly, a loud bang boomed and the ship jolted violently, nearly knocking them off their feet.

"You okay?" Aaron asked, catching hold of her.

"Yeah," said Chasmira shakily. "What the heck—?"

The ship jerked again, and they both crashed against the railing. Everything grew dark, cold, all at once, a shadowy iciness striking the air encompassing them. The stars rapidly faded, depriving them of all remaining light.

"Something is seriously wrong," muttered Aaron gravely. A loud, horrifying cry mingling a roar and screech permeated the air as a great head with terrible eyes, dark blue scales, and oozing fangs loomed up out of the water before them. It reared its head, lunging towards the ship a third time.

"C'mon!" Aaron grabbed Chasmira's hand. As they ran, the sea serpent rammed into the ship, knocking them harshly against the railing again.

Regaining their footing, they darted back into the ball room where madness prevailed as people yelled, screamed, falling all over each other in a wild panic.

"What's going on?" Aaron shouted to Rachel as they met up with her, Nathan, and Eric.

"Dunno. Some evil serpent thing crashing into the ship."

"They're getting everyone onto the life boats," Eric added. "We've all been ordered to go to the lower deck."

They all raced along with the crowds of anxiously murmuring people down to the lower deck. Aaron still clutched Chasmira's hand and he tightened his grasp as fleeing passersby knocked violently into them. He gripped so hard it hurt, but she said nothing, nor did she dare let go.

Eric glanced concernedly at her pale face, asking gently, "Are you okay?"

"Sure." She forced a feeble smile.

Soon they clambered into one of the life boats which lowered into the ocean.

As the wild waves tossed them, a thick rain suddenly poured down, drenching them all and rocking the waves even more violently.

"What happened to the serpent?" shouted Tiff over the tumult.

"I don't see him anymore!" yelled Eric. "I reckon he has something to do with the storm though. He's a leviathan, looks like."

"Why would a leviathan randomly attack our ship?" Rachel asked.

"He wouldn't. Something's up."

As they drifted further from the sinking ship, a look of dread and fear flashed across Chasmira's face.

"We'll be okay." Aaron squeezed her hand.

"It's not that."

"Then what is it?"

"Krystal and Josh. They're still in the ship—asleep—the sleeping powders—"

"But they're not in danger. I mean, they can't drown," sniffed Nathan. "I mean, they *are* fairies—"

Rachel snorted. "Don't be an idiot, Nathan. They could die a million other ways. You know, like, the pressure from the ship crushes them, they wake up, can't find their way out and starve to death—"

Aaron suddenly dove into the water and Chasmira followed.

"What are you two doing?!" shouted Rachel. "Neither of you swim that well! Oh, jiminy cricket, if you people would *listen*..."

Rachel dove in after them and, with her wide, skillful strokes, soon caught up.

"You all are crazy!" Nathan called after them. "Do you want me to come too?"

"No," Rachel called back. "You three stay there and keep an eye out for us."

"Okay!" Then he mumbled, "You're all still crazy," while Eric and Tiff watched on with concerned expressions.

Aaron and Chasmira grabbed Rachel as they reached the ship and flew up on deck. It was hard to keep one's footing as the deck slanted and a good portion of the ship sunk under water already.

"What now?" asked Rachel, gripping the railing.

"Follow me," said Aaron.

They followed him into the ship, racing down corridors and stairs, crashing into walls as the ship careened ominously.

"Our rooms were right at the bottom of this staircase—" Aaron began, but upon rounding the corner, they stopped short and stared in horror. The staircase already lay completely submerged.

The three looked at each other before diving down. They reached the bottom of the staircase, but the door was partly closed and jammed. As they resurfaced, Rachel said, "I think I'm small enough to squeeze through the opening. You two stay here and try to open the door further so Krystal and Josh can fit through, and I'll go get them."

Chasmira frowned, eyes flashing with vivid concern. "But you can't hold your breath that long, can you? Elves can't—"

Rachel presented a pendant from her pocket, holding it up. "Fifteen minutes. I knew water club would prove useful someday."

"Are you sure?" Aaron asked.

"I can do this."

"I know you can." Chasmira nodded. "We'll be praying."

"You just concentrate on that door." Rachel flung the pendant over her head, diving back down.

It was a tight fit, but she just managed to squeeze through the doorway. She knew exactly where Josh's and Krystal's rooms were—only two halls down, and their rooms weren't far from each other—but upon reaching Krystal's, she was faced with another problem. The door wouldn't budge, and, upon inspection, neither would Josh's. The pressure from the water forced them to stay closed. She must find something to bust them open. As she swam in search of something, she glanced at her watch. Five minutes passed already.

She swam a couple more long minutes before stumbling upon an axe. Why it lay in the floor of the hallway she did not know, but she gratefully hefted it, swimming back to Krystal's room and hacking at the door. Swinging a heavy axe while under water proved not the easiest thing to do, so Rachel made slow progress, but finally she butchered an opening in the door and swam through.

Krystal lay on her bed sleeping and snoring peacefully, air bubbles flying up from her nose. Rachel lifted her and paddled over to the door, shoved Krystal through, trying not scrape her against the jagged edges of lacerated door, then squeezed back through herself.

She carried Krystal back to the door which Chasmira and Aaron still tried to budge open.

"I'm laying Krystal here and going for Josh."

"Alright!" Chasmira offered a quick prayer, knowing Rachel did not have much time left, nor did they. The water crawled beyond the staircase.

Rachel quickly found Josh's room. Thankfully the door stood open wide, but inside, she saw no sign of Josh. She panicked for a second and then thought—the bathroom. Heading for the bathroom, she prepared herself, really hoping he wasn't taking a shower when he fell asleep, but as she swam inside, he lay fully clothed, sleeping peacefully in the bath tub. No time existed to wonder why he slept in the tub. In fact, less than a minute remained, so she grabbed Josh and made her way as fast as possible to the stair case. It was slow going with Josh being so heavy, but somehow she found the strength, making it back to the door which still hadn't budged.

Chasmira's eyes flared with panic. "We can't open it. How much time do you have left?"

"A few seconds."

"Is there anything down there you can use to break down the door or anything?"

"There's an axe. But I won't be able to hold my breath and swing it..."

Suddenly, the pendant's magic failed and Rachel's cheeks puffed out with air as she was forced to hold her breath.

"I have an idea!" Chasmira cried. "Get the axe, quickly!"

Rachel did so and returned to the door.

"Set it in the hallway, a few feet back from the door, then move out of the way!"

Rachel did as she was told then waited, hoping and praying Chasmira's idea would work fast.

Chasmira sank into the water, peered through the crack in the door, and spotted the axe. Forming a quick mental picture of it in her head, she swam as far from the door as possible, ordering Aaron to do the same. She hadn't completed such advanced levitation yet, but she hoped and prayed she would be able to do it. She concentrated, forming the axe in her mind, ordering it to lift up off the ground and—

Something suddenly scythed through the door at an amazing speed, creating a gaping hole as it crashed through.

"Woah, way to go, Cassy!" Aaron exclaimed in awe.

"Help me with this!" she ordered, lifting the axe.

Together, they tore a hole through the door big enough for Rachel to lift Krystal through.

"You next, Rachel. We'll get Josh."

Rachel swam quickly to surface and gasp a breath while Aaron and Chasmira hefted Josh out safely through the hole.

Rachel soon returned to help Chasmira carry Krystal while Aaron bore Josh over his shoulder, declaring, "Now, let's get out of here, fast."

Forced to swim as the water rose higher, they stroked as fast as they could with the two sleeping fairies, surfacing every so often so Rachel could catch her breath.

Soon the rooms lay completely submerged, but then the ballroom came in sight. They were close to freedom. Aaron led them out the window, and finally they surfaced outside.

"Now what?!" shouted Chasmira above the tumult of the lingering torrents of rain.

"Over there!" Aaron shouted. "I can see them!"

Very dimly in the distance and through the thick blankets of rain, they could make out the hazy shadows of a couple life boats.

"Hurry!" Chasmira panicked.

Yet to hurry when dangerous waves and winds swirled them every which way proved no easy thing to do, especially as they tried to hurry in a particular direction.

They all held hands to stay together, but Chasmira soon found her grasp slipping from Rachel's, and Rachel and Krystal swept away from them, their frantic cries swallowed by the merciless screams of the storm.

Josh drifted from Aaron's grasp. Soon only he and Chasmira remained together.

"Hold on!" he cried desperately, feeling her slipping away from him. to

"Cassy!"

The wind, rain, and roughness of the waves melted away just as the ballroom did when she first entered. She alone existed, yet her beauty was not the reality now flashing before him but rather her helplessness, accented by his own pathetic, helpless state. She fast became a small, white, screaming dot rippling away from him as though one of the waves themselves...

"Aaron!" she screamed. The waves forced them apart as the wind carried something in it sharp claws which hit Chasmira in the head, knocking her unconscious.

PART 2

CHAPTER 14

The young man slowly opened his eyes. Was it all a dream, an unfathomable nightmare? For a moment, he wished this, but he quickly renounced that wish. For if it had been a dream, then *she* was a dream as well, and the dance, those long, invaluable moments they cupped in their hands and hearts together. No, he felt glad it was not a dream. But then he thought that if she was real, so was the serpent and the storm, the memory of her drifting further and further from sight...

Eric sat up. His clothes were somewhat dried by the warm sun shining overhead, though a bit tattered. He looked around and found himself on a sandy beach. A forest lay not far behind.

Standing, he looked about. Where were the others? Had they survived? Were they here too, and furthermore, where *was* here?

Walking a little ways along the beach, he suddenly espied something in the distance. Treading closer, he saw it was some*one*, and stepping yet nearer, saw it was *her*.

He raced over, kneeling beside her. She lay sprawled on her back, soaking in the sun. She clearly just washed ashore for her body was still very wet. Blood trickled from a wound in her head. He must get her to safety, tend her wound, and, hopefully, he thought with a half dread and a half hope pounding simultaneously in his heart, manage to wake her up.

Gently picking her up, he carried her into the wood. He laid her under one of the trees, safe from the sun's hot rays, then tore the bottom of her skirt to create a bandage.

After tending the wound and building a fire so she would dry more quickly, he sat and waited, staring down at her. How beautiful she looked, how graceful, sweet, gentle, patient. How noble and queenly she appeared beyond the tattered, soiled gown, its sparkle now diminished. Yet the natural sheen of her spirit could not be quenched, reflected in the color slowly returning to her cheeks. An overwhelming urge to kiss that temptingly crimson cheek gripped him, but perhaps that wouldn't be right. She wasn't his, and he dare not tempt himself further. How he wished she *was* his, for he loved her almost from the moment they met. Then he shook his head. No, he must not allow such selfish thoughts to permeate. He should be grateful Amiel blessed him with her friendship, and he was. But maybe it wouldn't be so very wrong for him to kiss her hand.

So he gently took her small, slender hand in his and pressed it gently to his lips. An undeniable thrill rippled through him as her flesh brushed so gently against his own and a smile tugged at the corners of her mouth. Then, slowly, her eyes opened.

"Eric?" she rasped.

"Yes, I'm here." He squeezed her hand, gazing down intensely.

"What happened?"

"Our ship got caught in a storm."

"Oh, yes. I remember."

She suddenly sat up, glancing worriedly all about. "Where's Aaron? And Sarah? Rachel? All the others—?"

She fell back against the tree, grasping her head as the pain grabbed viciously.

"Shh..." Eric gazed at her comfortingly. "I don't know where they are, but I'm sure they've made it safely somewhere. Just rest for now. You hit your head somehow. Probably a piece of driftwood or something. You need to rest..."

As Chasmira closed her eyes and fell asleep again, Eric carefully changed her bandages. True, they were fresh enough, but just in case, he changed them. Besides, he no longer could resist the yearning to engage in that smallest yet most sacred bit of innocent contact...

In the evening, she awoke, eyes glinting with a far more alert gleam. She said too the pain in her head had subsided and that she was hungry. Both of these announcements pleased him.

"Here." Eric handed her some berries. "I found these nearby."

"How do we know they're not poisonous?"

"I've taken classes. I'm well-trained to detect such things. Besides," his eyes twinkled playfully, "I ate some this morning, and I'm still alive and kicking."

Chasmira smiled and tasted the berries, declaring them quite good, soon devouring the whole lot of them. Eric just sat watching her pensively and admiringly.

"Are you still hungry?" he asked when she finished.

"No. I'm quite full."

"Awe, that's too bad, 'cause we just caught a load of tasty fish," Josh's voice floated towards them and he suddenly entered the clearing along with—

"Aaron!" Chasmira exclaimed, hopping up, racing into his arms. He hugged her close. Eric watched on, both joy and sadness glinting in his eyes.

"We've been so worried," Chasmira sighed as they all sat down. "Have you seen the others?"

"No." Aaron shook his head.

"So, Josh, what about all that tasty fish?" Eric asked.

"Well, actually, we ate most of it. But you can have the leftovers."

He presented two small yet delicious looking trout that Eric and Chasmira shared.

As Chasmira sat finishing her fish, she kept looking up at Aaron, smiling. She felt half relieved and grateful that he was there, safe and sound, and at the same time half-worried that something else might happen any moment which would separate them again. Aaron's gaze flip-flopped between Chasmira's beautiful yet weary looking face and at Eric, at whom he stole brief glances every now and then before quickly turning away. Aaron's eyes did not once met Eric's, yet he felt Eric studying him at times. This knowing only made him feel all the more guilty and dread all the more what he must do.

Soon Chasmira grew sleepy, and with a final, faint smile, drifted off into a peaceful, dreamless sleep.

"Josh," Aaron whispered. "Can you watch Chasmira for a few moments?"

"Uhh, sure," Josh replied as both he and Eric looked at Aaron curiously.

"Eric, could I please have a word with you?" Aaron muttered, still averting Eric's eyes.

"Sure."

Aaron and Eric arose and walked off a few feet into the forest.

In a secluded place, they stopped, and Aaron looked up at Eric. How calm his bright, blue eyes shone. They held a glint of hurt but glimmered so calm and forgiving, making Aaron feel even more fault than he did already. He stared down at the ground guiltily like a school boy just caught cheating on a test.

"Look, Eric—"

"You don't have to say anything—"

"Yeah, I do. Look, I'm sorry I accused you of hitting on Chasmira."

"You would've been right."

"Yeah, but, well...you didn't know about us. I mean, technically, there wasn't exactly an 'us,' just a wishing of me for there to be one."

"It's okay.

Aaron looked up to see Eric smiling sincerely and holding out his hand.

"Truce?"

Aaron took his hand and shook it firmly, grinning in return. "Truce."

"So...uhh...out of curiosity, *is* there an 'us' now?"

Aaron stared at Eric perplexed.

"You and Chasmira, I mean," Eric added quickly.

"Oh, that. Yes, actually. I mean, we're not actually dating yet. I told her I wanted to move things slowly for now, and she was fine with that, but, yeah, we told each other how we felt, and, uhh, I guess we are technically a couple now."

Aaron beamed at the thought, an uncontrollable joy and unknown power suddenly gripping him. He never really had the chance to let it sink in before it's hard to think when a giant serpent is sinking your ship. But now that Eric mentioned it, well, it was nice, the thought of Chasmira being his girlfriend, even if it was only on a friends-only basis for now.

Eric smiled. "Good for you."

"Thanks. Should we get back now?"

"Sure."

Aaron led the way and Eric sighed deeply, glad that Aaron did not notice the sad glimmer surely reflected in his eyes, a gleam he could not conceal, that would certainly only cause further strain between the two of them.

Chasmira was awake again already, grinning as the two of them reentered.

"Hullo." Aaron sat besides her. "Have a nice nap?"

"Yes, very short, yet I do feel a bit more chipper now."

"I can't really sleep right now anyways. My thoughts and prayers keep flying to Sarah, Rachel, and all the others. I mean, do you think they ended up here too? And where exactly is 'here' anyways?"

"'Here' is the Prismatic Isle, and the others are all quite fine." As the woman whose voice spoke entered the clearing, they all stared and Chasmira took in her breath before exclaiming, "Labrier!"

"Yeah, and not to mention us," added Sarah as she and a good number of familiars strolled through the trees behind their History teacher.

CHAPTER 15

Everyone greeted each other, declaring their thankfulness at finding each other safe and sound. Labrier assured them everyone else from the ship made it safely to a nearby island and she would inform Mr. Root of their own safety at once.

They all gathered on the couch, chairs, and floor of the spacious living room of Labrier's roomy cottage, located not far inland from where Chasmira and the others met.

They sat by the warmth of the roaring fireplace, sipping hot chocolate—Labrier had slipped into the kitchen to fetch herself a mug of the warmly refreshing stuff—when a small, curious figure wandered in from the hallway.

He was a rabbit with chocolate-colored fur, standing on his hind legs and wearing an off-white night shirt from which the tips of his little brown toes stuck out. He stood rubbing his eyes quite groggily, having apparently just woken up.

"Oh, how cute!" squealed Sarah, turning to Labrier as she reentered, hot chocolate in hand. "I didn't know you had a pet rabbit—"

At this, the bunny suddenly seemed very awake, though no less cranky looking. Hopping right up to Sarah, he waved a front paw at her, retorting irritably, "I am *not* a pet, young lady! I am a rabbit of the noble Twitchy family, descendent of the renowned Miramar, and don't you forget it!"

Sarah stared at him incredulously, then muttered, "Well, excuse me..."

"Hush, Twitchy," Labrier said calmly as she sat in the rocker next to the fireplace. "Please control yourself around our guests..."

"Hmph. 'Guests,' are they? If they are guests, they should have common courtesy not to awaken the members of this household, and—" He paused to sniff Aaron, then crinkled his nose unpleasantly "—this one smells funny."

"Yep," Aaron whispered to Sam, "he's related to Miramar alright."

"Alastair Twitchy." Labrier's voice was sharp, sage eyes containing a hint of warning. "Kindly control yourself, will you?"

Alastair reluctantly sunk down on his hind quarters, but he crossed his arms and proceeded to look very sulky.

"Alastair—I like that name," Chasmira tried to cheer him up.

"Yes." The bunny straightened with an air of pride and dignity. "Alastair's my name, after the renowned healer, Alastair Lance."

"Alastair Lance!" Rachel exclaimed, as their eyes, sparkling with interest, turned to Labrier. "Oh, I've read all about him. Did you really know him?"

Labrier sighed, eyes gleaming with the happiness of memories long past. "Yes, I knew him. He was one of the greatest healers of that time, a great friend too..."

As Labrier reflected, Alastair snorted, "Well, if a bunny can't get some hot chocolate around here, I'm off to bed."

"Oh, forgive me, Twitchy. I'll get you some."

Labrier left to fetch him a mug, and when she returned, Josh quipped cheerfully, "Well, now that Labrier's found us all, I say we go visit my sister tomorrow. I mean, we may as well, right?"

He looked at Labrier with a hopeful glance that said he would much rather stay here than return to school.

But Labrier's face grew suddenly so starkly grave that Josh's blanched, as did all their faces. She cast a knowing look at Alastair who returned the glance and promptly excused himself along with his hot chocolate, hopping back to his bedroom.

As a complete hush fell across the room, Labrier gazed at them with all seriousness. "Josh, Chasmira, Aaron, everyone, the reason I've been here on the Prismatic Isle, the reason I left the school...Josh..." Repeating his name, she looked at him with such sorrowful eyes that penetrated each of their hearts with an icy blade, "I'm so sorry...Toby and Amanda Danielle...they're both dead..."

Amanda Danielle dead...dead, *dead...*

Her words seemed distant, they did not seem real, or at least...they *could not be real...* Everyone stared at her dumbfounded, Josh slowly shaking his head in bewilderment.

Labrier's voice seemed far away still, surreal, as she continued, "...their palace was attacked by some mysterious evil that's been growing for some time now. They gave their medallions to the twins so they would be protected, and then...they were killed. I saw it happen, they died saving their children..."

A sob choked Labrier's voice. She blinked her eyes very rapidly, trying to force back her tears.

Chasmira stared at the wall, its blankness reflecting the hole severed in her heart. She could not comprehend it. No, they could not have died. Not her beloved teacher and her courageous husband. Surely the couple hid somewhere, they would all see Amanda Danielle's smile, hear her laugh again. They would see Toby holding Amanda Danielle in his arms and kissing her in the sunlit garden...

Labrier's voice pierced her thoughts. "Come. I will take you to their tomb." Her voice was soft, and yet the very words seemed like cold steel striking Chasmira's very soul. *Their tomb*...Such eerily final words...So they really were...

Labrier led them in silence down the garden path until they came to a cavern of white stone, ivy scaling its every side. They entered the cave, and she led them down a series of torch-lit corridors and stairways, stopping before two, double stone doors.

"They're being preserved by magic. It was always their wish to be buried in their palace gardens. They're being kept here until everything returns to normal and they can be buried there in peace..."

Slowly, the doors slid open as Labrier touched them, stone scraping painfully against stone. Upon entering, they stopped short.

Chasmira gasped and clasped a hand over her mouth, as if trying to hold in the sobs that wanted so desperately to come.

Josh turned very white as his empty eyes gazed within.

Two white, stone tables stretched next to each other, and upon them lay Amanda Danielle and Toby. A light emanated gently from above to rest upon the precious couple. Slowly, almost reluctantly, they sidled towards the tables. They had to see, to know...they must try to grasp the awful reality so they could say "good-bye..."

Toby looked so pale yet so brave, handsome, kingly, even in death. His sword rested between his hands folded upon his chest. A strange, celestial glow radiated from him as the shafts of sad, heavenly light caused his hair to glow like strands of pure, white gold.

Then they forced themselves to look away and upon their beloved teacher. Chasmira's hand flew to her mouth again, Rachel gasped, Krystal bit her lip. They all stared down at her face, so pale, yet it held a queenly air. Her great beauty still clung to her, and as the light illuminated her face, she too bore a heavenly glow. A rose rested between her hands also folded upon her breast. A dove perched upon one of her slender shoulders, chorusing its mournful lullaby, nuzzling its queen softly with its beak. Chasmira's eyes drifted to her hair which flowed in shimmering curls about her face. It shimmered silver, as all fairies' hair when they die.

Suddenly, the shocking reality hit and Chasmira released a cry, weeping loudly, bitterly upon Aaron's shoulder. He placed his arm around her, tears streaming down his face as well. Sarah stood on the other side of Chasmira and began to stroke her hair, crying softly. Though she didn't know Amanda Danielle or Toby, she learned to love them, especially the beautiful fairy, from the stories Chasmira wrote her, and she knew how much Chasmira loved her too. Eric stood beside her, head bowed, tears trickling down his cheek as he prayed silently. Rachel gripped Nathan's hand as they both cried quietly, and Hailey sobbed, blowing her nose loudly on the tissue Sam gave her as he cried softly. Josh sank to the ground, sobbing uncon-trollably, and he half-whispered, half-choked: "Sis..." Krystal suddenly forgot every mean prank he ever pulled on her, kneeling beside him and placing her arms around him, trying to comfort him vainly with gentle words.

After some time passed—how much time, they did not know, for it seemed an eternal instant as they gazed down upon their beloved teacher—Labrier said, "Come. We should return." Her eyes were red with tears as well.

Everyone solemnly turned to exit the tomb, each casting one last glimpse at the king and queen. As Chasmira glanced at Amanda Danielle, it suddenly seemed as though she smiled, and Chasmira knew she beamed in Heaven. They would see her again someday, and she thanked Amiel for this comfort. A small consolation it seemed, and yet, it was a comfort none-the-less. Perhaps the others noticed too, for they all seemed to smile a bit at her before they made their way from the tomb.

Back inside the cottage, everyone silently brooded before the fire. Labrier made them all more hot cocoa which they reluctantly drank, especially Josh, who just stirred it idly with his spoon.

Then Labrier walked to the bookcase and took something out of a small, wooden box. Gliding over to Chasmira, Chasmira recognized it as her blue sapphire, the one Amanda Danielle took from her on their last meeting.

Labrier handed the warping stone to Chasmira. "She left a note saying I was to give this to you..."

"Why did she take it?" Aaron scowled. "She knows we would've come and helped her. We would've been safe with our medallions. She told us to always keep them with us, and we have—"

"Yes," Chasmira interrupted. "And she knows too that there's not one of us who wouldn't have given up our medallions to save her and Toby. Don't you see...She loved us so much...she was protecting us...she knew we'd be willing to die to save her and Toby, she didn't want that..."

Labrier nodded. "True. The love of Amanda Danielle and Toby burned so vividly they would not have let anyone sacrifice their lives in their place..."

She exhaled a deep, sorrowful sigh and they all fell silent again.

After another, long moment, Labrier said, "Enough words have been spoken to-night. There are further important matters to be discussed, but I think that this is enough for now. Come I will show you to your bedrooms for the night."

Labrier's cottage contained loads of rooms so that two of them shared a bed-room. They wondered if the apparent abundance of space was some magic of Lab-rier's. The cottage certainly didn't appear so big on the outside.

But their thoughts lingered with Mrs. Daniels and Toby, the lifeless forms still haunting their minds. Together they prayed to find a little comfort in their grief then climbed into their cozy beds to settle into peaceful dreams where they could forget the day's sorrows until morning.

CHAPTER 16

It was late at night. Chasmira had wept softly into her pillow for hours, hoping to cry herself to sleep, but sleep cruelly refused to grant its blessing.

Finally, she arose to take a walk outside, silently tip-toeing from the room. Although subconsciously at first, she soon found herself wandering towards the garden and the tomb.

Chasmira touched the stone as Labrier did and it slid aside.

Inside was completely dark except for a solitary torch lit on one wall. Using her levitation skills, she made the torch to float before her, lighting the way. Slowly, she walked until she found herself before the tomb's door. Opening it and taking a deep breath, she stepped through.

As she saw their bodies lying on the white stone tables, the slanted beams of light falling from the ceiling illuminating them with a pale, ghostly, though yet angelic hue, she almost wished she hadn't come. Yet she could not go back. A voice inside told her she must go on.

Countless minutes passed as she sat next to Amanda Danielle, holding the cold hand in one of her own, brushing away tears with the other. Gazing down upon the peaceful face, she became lost in the memories of the time spent with her beloved teacher: her wonderful poetry lessons, over-the-glasses glares at Josh, especially after he stole their poetry assignment, song-like voice relating to them hers and Toby's story, the two of them declaring their eternal love in the garden by the school. A short yet wondrous time.

A soft, gentle cooing startled Chasmira from her reverie. The dove returned, caressing Amanda Danielle's other hand with its soft head. Chasmira smiled. How Amanda Danielle was loved by even the simplest creatures of her kingdom.

Yet something was different about the dove. It did not cry nor even seem sad as earlier. Its cooing grew louder as it nudged Amanda Danielle's hand then began to peck the soft flesh.

"Hey, stop that!" cried Chasmira, shooing the bird away and grasping the hand the bird pecked at. As she took the hand though, she gasped, nearly releasing it then holding on tight. It felt warm. No, perhaps she only imagined it. She decided to check both hands. Indeed, the right hand was warm like that of a person whose life still pumps within them. Slowly, she stepped back in disbelief, barely daring to hope. The dove flew over to Toby, nudging his right hand as well. It was warm too as Chasmira checked it. Something, or perhaps Someone told Chasmira hope still existed, and she burst from the tomb, shouting, "Labrier! Labrier, come quick!"

As she entered the cottage, shouting excitedly, Labrier rushed with the others down the stairs.

"What is it, child?" Labrier's eyes flashed concerned trouble.

"Labrier, everyone, I think—I think Amanda Danielle and Toby are still alive."

Labrier stared at her incredulously, and then, as if some great possibility suddenly dawned in her mind, took in a sharp breath and flew from the cottage and towards the tomb, the others following swiftly behind.

Into the tomb they raced, quickly to the burial room. Labrier grasped Amanda Danielle's right hand, turning it over in hers, then did the same to Toby's, then went back to Amanda Danielle.

"Come." Her voice quivered with scarcely contained excitement. "Come here and see."

They all crowded around and Labrier carefully turned over Amanda Danielle's hand, revealing her palm.

"A scar," breathed Aaron.

"What does it mean?" Josh's eyes bulged in hopeful awe.

"It means they are—in fact—still alive."

They all stared at her with wild, excited eyes, and Josh exclaimed, "Then it's not too late! Then you can make some potion and wake them up or something!"

Labrier shook her head, the light in her eye shadowed, though not so much as before.

"I'm afraid it's not that simple. Come, let's go back to the cottage, and I will explain all."

They silently left the tomb, yet not so hopelessly as when they departed earlier that day. How quickly and drastically the tides changed, as though they stepped back and watched the scene over many days, weeks, or months as opposed feeling such contrasted emotions within a few hours. Josh was the last to leave and cast a final hopeful glance at his sister, offering a quick, hopeful prayer.

Once back inside the cottage, they all settled around the fire in the living room, some on the floor, others on the couch or chairs, listening intently as Labrier explained:

"Amanda Danielle and Toby were attacked by one of the darkest types of magic—Shadow magic. It should've killed them in an instant, and, indeed, we all thought it did. Such powerful evil can only be countered by the great healers of the Kalvyrie Council, the makers of the medallions. Amanda Danielle and Toby knew their children would need the medallions in order to be saved, but they must've each cut their hands with one of the medallions, releasing just enough of its protective powers into them to spare their lives.

"But they are not free from danger yet. The magic they received from the medallions was small and will last only for a time. For how long, I know not. Thus, their lives are still in great danger."

"What can we do?" Josh's eyes flashed with a determined fire. The same flame flared steadily in the eyes of all present.

"The only way to break the dark curse flowing through their veins is to destroy the source of the curse. All we know is that the enemy hails from some world of his or her own dark making. Hints of the portal's entrance have been found. You must find the secret portal that leads to the enemy's fortress, and you must destroy him.

"Eric, Sarah, I give you these."

She drew from the folds of her skirt two medallions and handed one to each of them. They thanked her and donned them solemnly.

"Aaron," Labrier turned to him, "I place you in charge."

Aaron started. "Me?"

"Yes."

"Why must I lead—why not someone else—?"

"Because Amanda Danielle left me a note announcing that after hers and Toby's deaths—yes, she wrote 'deaths', as she and Toby could not have been sure that the cutting would spare them—that I was to summon you all here, and that she chose you, Aaron, to lead everyone to the enemy's fortress and destroy him. She appointed you to this task.

"That explains too why the serpent attacked your ship, and the storm. The enemy must've found out you were on your way to Prismatic. I figured those things were works of his dark magic, which is why I intervened with my own magic and made sure you ended up on this Island."

"When do we start out?" asked Aaron, not so eager as a few seconds ago before Labrier appointed him leader.

"Tomorrow morning. All I can tell you is that the portal is said to be hidden somewhere in the western woods. Also, I would advise you not to tarry, not to waste time. I do not know how much time they have left.

"For now, I advise you all to get a good night's sleep. You have a long journey before you."

They all bid her "good-night" then slowly dispersed to their rooms, talking amongst themselves about the adventure awaiting them tomorrow and congratulating Aaron on being appointed leader, encouraging him. Even Krystal and Sarah offered encouragement, if skeptically.

Chasmira was last to leave before Aaron, and she placed a hand on his shoulder. "She's right, you know. If Amanda Danielle placed you in charge, it's for a good reason. Besides, I know from personal experience what a great leader you are. Have faith. We'll find the portal."

He smiled weakly and she slipped to bed. His dismal smirk quickly faded though. A doubtful, queasy feeling of dread grasped his stomach, and this time her words did nothing to qualm that feeling.

He did not go to bed along with the others. In fact, he was still sitting and staring into the fire pensively, lines of worry etched upon his brow, when Labrier entered the room.

"Aaron?"

He spun around, startled.

"Oh, hello, Miss Labrier."

She sat beside him on the rug.

"What is it, Aaron? What's troubling you?"

"Nothing..." he mumbled, then sighed. "Actually...it's just...I can't understand why Mrs. Daniels would place me in charge. I mean, I'm just afraid, I guess. What if I mess everything up? Lead us all wrong? What if we never find the portal and she and Toby..?" His voice faded. He could not bring himself to utter the dreadful word.

"Aaron," Labrier spoke in a voice both gentle and commanding. "Do you remember what Amanda Danielle often said, about not having to fear others if we know Amiel is on our side?"

"Yes. But still...I wish...couldn't you come with us?" Aaron looked up at her with a small glimmer of hope, though he himself knew the answer.

"No, I must stay here and watch over Amanda Danielle and Toby."

She gazed deeply into his eyes as if searching his very thoughts. "It is true that there will be no Amanda Danielle to grant you wisdom along the way this time, and I know it is a daunting task. But she left you in charge for a reason, Aaron. She trusts you. And I trust you to recall and use the wisdom she has already given you. Do it for her, Aaron. She knows and I know that you can and will make a good leader, if you will let Amiel make you into one. I offer you now one last piece of advice: a good leader always listens to the council of his friends. While all final decisions rest in your hands, remember to ask your friends for guidance, and they will gladly give it.

"Now, let us pray together."

After they prayed, both for Amanda Danielle and Toby, as well as strength and wisdom for all of them, including Aaron as he led the morrow's quest, Aaron felt more at ease, the doubt in his mind replaced with peace.

Labrier retired to bed while Aaron sat gazing into the fire, still deep in thought over the adventures tomorrow might bring.

Presently, he heard a creak on the stairs and looked up. To his surprise, Sarah entered the living room.

"Hey."

"Hey."

An awkward silence followed, but then Sarah took a deep sigh and rolled her eyes. "Look. I know we've never been on the best of terms, but...look, I don't wanna go out on some big, important mission with us quarreling, okay? I mean, Chasmira really likes you, and, well, I guess you're not so annoying as you used to be. Besides, if Labrier put you in charge, well...I just want you to know I'm behind you all the way."

She did not speak in a very heart-felt voice, but he knew she meant it and that it was hard to say. So he smiled. "Thanks. And I'll try not to be so...'annoying."

"Okay. Truce, then?"

"Truce." He extended his hand.

"Uh-uh." Sarah shook her head. "Shaking hands is going *way* too far. Last time I touched your hand, we were twelve and you were pulling me behind a bush heavens-knows-why, and it was all clammy and..." She shuddered. "Terrible memories..."

Aaron laughed and lowered his hand. "Alright then. But we have a truce anyways, right?"

"Right." Then she stood and announced, "Well, I'm off to the bathroom. Good night."

"'Night."

She started for the hallway but then paused, a sly smile creeping over her face. "Oh, and if you DO ever get on my nerves too much, well, just remember I'll be there to impersonate you and get you into detention once we return to school."

Aaron laughed again. "I'll be sure not to forget."

CHAPTER 17

They started out early in the morning.

As Aaron led them through the western woods, they all chatted gaily amongst themselves—well, some more gaily than others. Josh described the nightmare he dreamt last night—something about being chased by a giant tuna, but the chocolate-covered butterfly came to his rescue. Krystal mumbled about not being able to wear makeup for a week as she lost all hers in the shipwreck, while Rachel wished for a good book to read. Other than these mild complaints, they were all content enough and enjoyed traversing the beauty of the Prismatic Woods.

At noon, they stopped to rest besides a small stream and eat some bacon and beans for lunch, which Rachel claimed made up for the lack of books. Krystal, on the other hand, remained quite perturbed. She kept looking at her reflection in the mirror and muttering how wretched she looked. Tiffany tried to comfort her, but all to no avail.

They were just packing up, about to start off again, when suddenly they heard a soft cooing.

"Did you hear that?" Hailey asked.

"Yeah." Eric scanned the trees. "What was it?"

The cooing resounded again and Sam suddenly took in his breath dramatically.

"What? What?" Nathan asked and they all looked at him curiously.

"It sounded like the rare cooing herb," Sam breathed excitedly, and hopeful animation sprang into Hailey's eyes.

Josh shook his head. "Uhh, hate to disappoint you herb-lovers but, uhh, it's just a bird."

Sam suddenly looked very disappointed and Hailey cast Josh a nasty look.

They all looked up into one of the trees where a beautiful white dove perched, staring down at them with bright, inquisitive eyes.

"I think it's the dove that was at Amanda Danielle's tomb," breathed Chasmira. "The one that showed me she was still alive."

The dove bobbed its head as if in confirmation then took flight to another tree a few feet away. They followed it.

"I think she's trying to tell us something," Rachel said. "It's like she's trying to show us the way or something."

Krystal frowned skeptically. "It's a *bird*."

"No, look." Aaron shook his head. "Look at her eyes. They're so deep and thoughtful. I really think she understands us. She's trying to help us."

Krystal rolled her eyes. "Well, *you've* finally fallen off your rocker..."

"No, I agree, I think we should follow her," Eric claimed.

"Me too." Chasmira looked up at the dove and asked gently, "Dove, can you show us the way to Rorrim's portal? Do you really understand us? Can you show us the way?"

The dove crooned softly and bobbed its head three times.

"See." Chasmira turned back too the rest of them. "I say we follow her."

"It *is* the only clue we've got," Nathan shrugged. "May as well."

"It's Aaron's choice, though, remember?" Hailey reminded. "Labrier put him in charge."

All eyes turned upon Aaron inquisitively, as if in expectation of some great wisdom. An uneasiness settled upon his heart as they depended upon what they surely anticipated to be the right choice. After a moment's thought, he fumbled, "Umm, alright then, I think you're all right. We follow her. Lead on, dove."

The dove cooed once more then took wing, swooping to another tree several yards away.

"I don't believe we're following a bird," Krystal muttered. "And how do we know it's a 'her', anyways—ouch!"

Krystal looked up as she felt a sharp pecking on her head. The dove hovered above, casting her a sharp look.

"Oh, yeah," Josh, smirked. "That's a girl for you. She's a got a temper like you as well, Krystal. How about that? Besides, she looks like a girl anyways with that beautiful plumage."

Krystal sent him a look that said how *dare* he complement a bird when he never called *her* pretty, and that he best be quiet or *she'd* be pecking *him* in the head next.

* * *

After a day's travels, they had journeyed deep into the western woods. Trees stretched endlessly on all sides. Nothing else lay in sight for miles.

They all settled down to make camp for the night, the girls preparing beans and the remainder of their bacon stock. Originally, they brought more bacon, but Nathan tried to cook it for lunch and only succeeded in burning it miserably, nearly reducing it to cinders. Rachel proceeded not to talk to him all day, and every time he made a move towards the pack containing the bacon, she cast him such a nasty glare that he dare not even think about trying to prepare the night's supper. He even refused to eat any more of the bacon.

After eating, they settled down around the fire for a nice rest from the day's travels. Nathan and Josh decided to make use of some pebbles they found to play a nice game of marbles. Josh quickly grew agitated as Nathan kept accidentally bouncing them off his head and stormed off to see what Hailey and Sam were doing.

"We're inspecting a strange sort of herb," Hailey whispered as she and Sam crouched even lower on the ground, sinking as close to the vibrating plant as possible.

"It appears to be a rare sort of snoring herb..."

"Or it's probably just the wind," Josh muttered, shrugging.

Hailey cast him a deathly glare before returning her full focus to the herb, and Josh resolved to go join the others around the fire.

"Well," Rachel was saying. "At least we have left-over bacon for breakfast."

"Yep." Chasmira shrugged. "Then that'll be the last of it."

"How are we doing on supplies, Cassy?" Aaron asked.

"Oh, we have plenty for several days. Labrier *did* say that it was only a three day journey to the portal, right?"

"Yup. Three days into the western woods. I'd say we're off to a good start, thanks to our new friend up there."

They all glanced up at the dove. Chasmira almost thought it blushed.

"And thanks to our good leader," Eric added.

"Yeah, well, when Labrier put me in charge, I admit I was sort of skeptical."

"Tell me about it," Krystal mumbled, while Sarah stifled a laugh.

"But thank Amiel, I think this mission is going to turn out to be easier than we thought, especially with the dove."

"Yes, thank Amiel for that dove." Chasmira lowered her head in a humble nod. "Though once we reach the portal, who knows what dangers lay in store..."

"Well yes, but let's not get ahead of ourselves," Eric said. "One thing at a time."

"Yup," Aaron sighed contentedly. "One thing at a time. For now, we just relax and enjoy a nice quiet walk in the woods for the next two days. It'll be a piece of cake...Mmm...chocolate cake..."

CHAPTER 18

Chasmira slowly opened her eyes, blinking in the bright sunlight streaming through the flap of the girls' tent.

Looking around, she saw that Krystal too sat blinking with half-open eyes, her hair totally a mess. Chasmira choked down a laugh. How appalled Krystal would be if only she could see herself.

Hailey and Sarah still completely snuggled beneath their covers beside Rachel who yet snored loudly.

After pulling her hair back, Chasmira made her way outside where the delightful smell of bacon and eggs wafted on the morning breeze to greet her.

The boys already sat around the fire, Josh wrapped up in his blanket and sharing much of the same half-awake expression Krystal bore.

Chasmira plopped between Aaron and Eric. "Good morning."

"Morning," Eric and Aaron said half-heartedly while Sam cheerfully replied, "Good morning, Miss Eriz, and how are you?"

The other boys glared at him as if it were inhuman to act so genuinely awake and gleeful at dawn, and Chasmira returned, "Fine, Sam. And you?"

"Oh, quite well. Though Josh on the other hand..."

Chasmira smiled at the groggily moaning Josh. "Not sleep well, Josh?"

"Nightmare. Watermelon bubblegum...rolling pins..."

"Sounds...terrible..." Chasmira snorted between forced-back fits of laughter.

"Terrible, question mark?" Eric whispered to her, and she had to stifle a giggle.

"Yeah, man, awful," Josh droned. "Thankfully I was saved by the smell of bacon..."

Presently, Hailey and Krystal joined them, Krystal looking as groggy as Josh, Hailey chipper as Sam.

Sam beamed brightly. "Good morning, Miss Bodiford, Miss Smith—"

"Oh, hang your greetings. Must you be so happy?" snapped Aaron.

Sarah presently joined them. "A bit cranky are we this morning?"

"You'd be cranky too if you slept next to 'bubble-gum man' all night. Kept kicking me..."

"Hey," sniffed Josh. "You'd be kicking too if a giant wad of bubblegum was trying to club you over the head with a rolling pin..."

"Good morning, sleepy-head," Chasmira greeted as Rachel glided in.

"Morning," she mumbled, sitting as far away from all of them as she could. They girls cast each other curious glances. Chasmira frowned. How unfriendly she looked. She usually fought Hailey for a seat next to Chasmira. Sarah wondered at never seeing Rachel so unawake in the morning. Usually, she was the one throwing pillows at Sarah to wake her up for school. Krystal only glared at Rachel whose hair and clothes were arranged far more neatly than Rachel usually took time for, especially out in the wilderness. And Hailey silently disapproved of the uncommonly haughty expression upon Rachel's face.

They all stared at her curiously ~~in silence~~, then continued talking and eating. All but Rachel.

"Hey, Rache, whatcha waiting for?" Nathan asked finally. "You love bacon."

"I'm not hungry." She shrugged her shoulders. A very uninterested look masked her face.

Her reply caused everyone's eyes to shoot in her direction. Even Josh and Krystal sat wide awake now, Krystal accidentally letting fly surprised jet of streams from her eyes which Tiff narrowly dodged as she emerged from her tent.

As Aaron nearly choked on his eggs, coughing loudly, Hailey said, "Well, maybe she doesn't feel well."

"I'm fine, thank-you." Rachel sat up perfectly straight, folding her hands neatly in her lap. Aaron stared harder, the fork clattering to the ground.

"Well...umm...would you like something to read while we finish breakfast?" Chasmira frowned, brow furrowed in deep concern.

"No, no. I find reading a dull hobby," Rachel answered.

"What the heck is wrong with you, Rachel?!" Aaron blurted out.

Rachel stared at him as if appalled, astounded, or taken aback, blinking at him silently as if he was the most stupid creature on the planet. "There is nothing at all wrong with me, and for your information, you rude, rude man, my name is not Rachel. It is Camille."

Everyone gawked at her, trying to fathom what they heard and struggling to decide what to say next. But suddenly someone emerged from the girl's tent, shrieking. It was Rachel. Or was it? She stared at the Rachel sitting by the fire.

"And I thought *one* was bad," Aaron whispered to Nathan and Eric.

"So, how do we tell who's the real one?" Sam asked.

The standing Rachel first gaped in complete disbelief and shock, then exclaimed, "Jiminy cricket!"

"Oh, yeah, that's her," said Nathan.

The fake Rachel stared at the real Rachel and asked, "Excuse me, but what do you mean by calling me a cricket? And don't you know it is impolite to stare, you rude, rude girl?"

"Here." Krystal handed the fake Rachel her cracked compact mirror.

"What—?" she shrieked as she gazed at her reflection, then blushed madly.

"Forgive me. I'm a shape-shifter, and I must've mumbled something in my sleep and turned into...Well, anyway, allow me to change back..."

She mumbled a few words and before them sat a maid with dark skin and luxious, long waves of dark hair. Her eyes gleamed a deep, alluring blue. She sat clad in a simple, light-weight, silky, white dress that fluttered in the slight breeze like wisps of clouds. The boys found themselves ogling, but Eric snapped out of his reverie as he asked, "But who *are* you?"

"Yeah..." Josh breathed. "Who *is* she..?"

As Krystal thumped Josh on the head, the maiden continued, "I am Camille. I was a captive of Rorrim. I overheard that heroes were in the land, so I escaped and tried to find them. I apologize for falling asleep in your tent, Rachel, but—"

"Rorrim?!" Rachel blurted out. "*Again*?! Well, at least we can say he's persistent..."

"That's impossible." Chasmira grew pale. "We defeated Rorrim—he's dead."

Camille shook her head. "Rorrim wished to be immortal. He sealed a piece of his spirit inside some sort of protective object. Through that he survives and grows more powerful."

Aaron eyed her cautiously. "And why should we trust one who knows so much about our greatest enemy?"

"Because I am the only person you know who's been there. I can show you the way to Rorrim."

"We already have a guide." Sam nodded towards the dove who lighted on Chasmira's shoulder.

Camille gazed the bird in the eye with a sharp glint in her own, replying coolly, "Deceit is now your greatest enemy. How can you know that this bird is not a foe? Seemingly harmless, yes, but looks can be misleading...besides, *I* can offer you proof."

Suddenly, something appeared in her hand and they stared. A medallion just like their own.

"Is this proof enough?" She gave them each a challenging look, deep, dark eyes flickering intensely.

"I suppose," Aaron said slowly. "Yet, the dove..."

"Can offer you know proof. For all you know, it could be leading you into a trap. But *I* can show you the way."

Aaron stared at the medallion, deep in thought, before turning to the others. "What do you think?"

This time though, no guidance was offered as they all gazed upon him hopefully, trusting, only Chasmira saying quietly, "You're the leader, Aaron. It's your choice."

For a moment, Aaron's stomach lurched as the words sunk in. His choice. Up until now, he'd had no real choice to make. A new pressure weighed upon him, a new uncertainty crept into his mind. He must make a choice, make one now. He glanced at his friends who gazed upon him with solemnity, anticipation, and confidence, then at the dove who seemed to stare at him with a sharp, steady, almost foreboding glare, as if trying to warn him. And yet, what if Camille was right? He turned to her deep, dark, sharp eyes for a few moments, then returned his gaze to the medallion. Yes, the medallion was proof, wasn't it? Didn't they hold more hope in trusting a real person, someone who'd actually been to Rorrim's Fortress, actually knew the way, actually bore their symbol? Doubt and confusion swirled in his mind. Whatever path he chose, the choice would prove irreversible, and though he felt one part of his mind telling him to say "no," the other part urged "yes," and in the end, the latter part triumphed...

"Yes, we will follow you," Aaron said, far more certainly than the nagging doubt erupting in his heart caused him to actually feel, the doubt he struggled quickly to suppress.

Chasmira closed her eyes a moment and drew a deep breath. She and the others cast each other glances flickering with uncertainty. But what could they say? Either choice seemed difficult and could lead to certain triumph or quick demise...

"Very well, then," Camille flashed a triumphant smile of perfectly white, straight teeth. "Shall we start out now?"

"Yes." Aaron nodded then turned to the others. "Let's pack up and head out."

While they all moved to complete their various tasks, Aaron quickly glanced from Chasmira's uncertain gaze and looked up at the dove. "I'm sorry. We won't be needing your services anymore. Thanks for everything. You're free to go."

The dove cast him a final, deeply meaningful look, one that punctured Aaron's heart, the doubt trying to force its way through the wound created there. Then the bird took flight.

A soft, comforting hand slipped into his, a soft voice saying, "You have chosen well, my leader."

Chasmira? No, it was not her voice. He looked up. Camille. For a moment his dark brown eyes locked on hers. They shimmered midnight blue, nearly black, reflecting so calmly, surely, that he felt drawn to them, somehow felt a hint of some euphoric release as he gazed into them. She smiled.

He quickly turned away and pulled back his hand. "I'll go put out the fire," he mumbled, strolling over to the dying flames.

Camille smiled a triumphant, brilliantly enchanting smirk. Chasmira stared a moment longer from the flap of her tent before slipping back inside to gather her things.

CHAPTER 19

Chasmira's stare was deep, solemn, thoughtful as she gazed out at the woods.

After hesitating a few moments, Eric strolled over. "Hey."

Snapping out of her thoughts, she smiled at him feebly. "Oh, hey."

"What's on your mind?"

The false smile quickly vanished. "Camille. Eric...do you trust her? Because if you do, then maybe I'm just being jealous and foolish, but the other girls are suspicious too—"

Eric took her hand. "You're right. There is something about her I don't like. I think we should talk to Aaron."

"But when? Camille's always around—"

"Right now," hissed Hailey's voice as she seemed to appear from no where.

"I've been shrinking myself and spying on her. She goes every evening to find some lake to bathe in. She'll be gone at least an hour."

Chasmira glanced at Eric who nodded. "No time like the present. Let's go rally everyone."

* * *

Everyone clustered around the blazing fire. Dusk fell and the first stars began to twinkle above them, fronds extending with a mocking sort of innocent, child-like wonder.

"So, what're we talking about again?" asked Aaron.

"Camille," Eric said. "We don't trust her."

Josh snorted. "Yeah, she's off her rocker if you ask me."

"She's a dunderhead," Hailey said in her matter-o-fact tone.

"Woah, wait, back up a bit." Aaron frowned. "Why would you have any reason to distrust her? I mean, she has a medallion, doesn't she?"

"She could've stolen it for all we know," Rachel sniffed. "The girl's clearly got issues..."

Aaron's eyes quickly grew agitated. "But she's done nothing to hurt us. She's only been helping us."

"Aaron, she came out of the blue to help us." Chasmira's eyes flickered with torment. "She has that look in her eye...I just have a bad feeling about her. We all do. Did not Miss Labrier warn us to watch who we put our trust in?"

"And yet you guys put your trust in a bird?" Aaron returned.

"At least the bird was leading us west." Chasmira frowned, growing agitated herself. "Camille's going north—"

"She knows where she's going—"

"How do we know that? Miss Labrier said we were to go west! Not north, not northwest, but *west*! And then you just let some stranger waltz in and tell us otherwise? I mean, what would Mrs. Daniels say if she were here, Aaron? Do you really think she'd like us following this Camille person?"

That struck a painful nerve and Aaron fell silent, defeated for a moment, but the stubbornly defensive look still flickered hotly in his dark eyes.

"That's right." Josh's eyes flashed dangerously. "This isn't about you. It's about my sister. Try thinking of someone besides yourself in this."

"Hey, I *am* thinking about your sister." Aaron's dark spheres blazed at him.

"Yeah, right!" Josh's face reddened, growing hot. "That Camille's blown your ego so out of proportion—that's all you think about is following her, pleasing her. She could be leading us into a trap for all we know, but you don't care. You don't give a hoot about if we're ever actually going to save my sister—"

"That's not true!" Aaron leapt to his feet.

"Yeah, right!" Josh sprang up, the veins in his forehead bulging passionately. "You're too stubborn to see it, but clearly my sister's left this mission in the hands of a selfish, stuck-up jerk!"

Aaron and Josh lunged at each other, but Eric quickly hopped up between them and held out his arms, holding them back.

"Enough! We won't get anywhere by fighting. I think we all need to retire to our tents or wherever, calm down, think things through, then regroup and discuss this..."

"Oh, hello." Camille cheerily glided into their midst. "What's going on? I hope I wasn't interrupting anything." She frowned concernedly.

Josh cast a final dark glare and scowl at Aaron before brushing past and storming into the tent. The others too rose and dispersed, except for Aaron who remained by the fire.

"Aaron?" Camille innocently placed a hand on his shoulder.

"Go away," he snapped, pulling away. "Please, just give me some time alone to think..."

Camille at first stood taken aback. But then she left, a slightly worried yet determined, angry flash in her eye. Yet, as she walked, that vicious gleam slowly disintegrated to be replaced with one cool, collected, and even more victoriously determined.

* * *

Aaron sat pondering, gazing into the fire for a couple hours, his mind nearly consumed by the war waging there. Were the others right? Had they any reason to doubt Camille? His thoughts were interrupted as someone's shadow stood over him. He looked up into Camille's face as she flashed her blinding teeth in a radiant smile, eyes glittering like dark, seductive gems.

"May I sit here?"

"Sure."

She sat on the log beside him.

"You seem troubled."

Aaron shrugged his shoulders.

Camille inched a little closer. "Care to tell me what's wrong?"

Aaron tensed as he felt her arm slide across to his far shoulder, the other delicate yet strong hand reaching up as her fingers crept along his body, sending sparks of that same, euphoric high coursing through him. He tried half-heartedly to suppress the effects of those sparks, but his feeble defense crumbled as her hands began to gently massage the tender spot between his shoulders and neck.

She sidled yet closer until she sat right next to Aaron, her warm, soft body pressed close against his. He swooned with the ecstatic pleasure of her scent, the feel of her heat, her soft curves, the euphoria steadily mounting as his heart leapt higher and higher within him. His skin was fire as she touched one hand to his cheek, turning his face towards hers. Her dark, gleaming eyes gazed right into his, captivating. The scent of fresh flowers from her perfume nearly overwhelmed him. For a moment, a discomfort grasped him as he studied her midnight eyes, and his own eyes darted to the fire, but some nameless shape seemed to leap up in the flames. Startled, he returned his gaze to Camille.

"You're a very strong, intelligent, handsome young man," she said in barely a whisper. His eyes again darted to the fire, and as the flames leapt up, he jumped once more. Chasmira's face flashed before him in the fire, hair waving in the golden flames, eyes blazing warningly. Was it some kind of sign? *Aaron, please, I'm you're best friend, I've never steered you wrong, please listen...* The flames seemed to plead...

Which voice should he listen to?

"Aaron," Camille's silky voice crooned firmly as she pivoted his face to meet hers once more.

"You're the leader. You're the one Labrier appointed. Don't let them push you around; *you* make the choices. Trust me, Aaron..."

The longer her dark eyes gazed into his, the further he pushed that first voice into the back of his mind, the further the echoing voice of the flames seemed to recede into distant nothingness, until only her voice, her presence, her power, consumed his every sense.

* * *

Chasmira couldn't sleep.

She must try, just one more time. It may very well prove all in vain, yet, all the same, she had to try to talk to Aaron again.

"Aaron? Are you in there?" she called softly into the boys' tent.

Aaron emerged.

"Yeah, I'm here," he said quickly.

"I didn't wake you, did I?"

"No. The others are asleep, but I've been up."

"Okay. Umm...can I talk to you about something?"

"Look, if this is about Camille—"

"Actually, it is." Chasmira felt herself growing agitated already.

Aaron rolled his eyes, sighing loudly.

"Look, Chasmira." He turned from her accusing gaze. "I—"

"Aaron, I think we should get rid of her," Chasmira said firmly.

Aaron stood silent a few moments, staring icily at the ground before turning slowly towards her as if an idea suddenly dawned upon him.

"You're jealous, aren't you?" he said slowly, lowly, eyes narrowing as embers began to flicker in them.

"What?"

"You're jealous of Camille."

"What—no—that's insane—!"

"How does it feel now that the shoe's on the other foot, Chasmira?" he sneered.

Chasmira blinked, dumbfounded.

"Aaron, this has nothing to do with—Aaron, she's dangerous! Do you hear yourself? She's tearing us apart—all of us! She's turning you against us, against *me*—"

"Shut-up, Chasmira! I'm the leader and I know what I'm doing. Labrier put *me* in charge, remember? Me, not you, not anyone else. Me! And we're going to do thing *my* way! And if that means following Camille, then so be it!"

Chasmira just stared at Aaron for a moment, her eyes flashing first with shock, then horror, then melting into a sort of vacant numbness, growing starkly cool. "Very well then, 'Master' Aaron. Have it your way." She wheeled, heading back to her tent.

As Aaron entered his tent, slouching down on his pillow, tired from his little outburst, he felt that twinge of guilt return. He never yelled at Chasmira like that.

Oh well. He had bigger things to worry about right now than some childish whim of Chasmira's. Tomorrow they would arrive at Rorrim's fortress.

CHAPTER 20

They traveled on in solemn silence the next day. Words were exchanged only between Camille and Aaron. The only other communication included icy stares between Josh and Aaron. The others did not even glance at him, nor he at them. The only one who seemed at all content was Camille, who, though she tried to conceal it, bore a triumphant twinkle in her eyes that Chasmira could not help but notice and loathe.

She led them deeper and deeper into the northwestern woods. The trees grew thick, their bare branches netted together like a vast web of cruel, grey, shadowy fingers above them, fingers which shielded even the grey light, letting hardly anything in, not even a breeze. Or, some thought gloomily, letting hardly anything out.

It was noon—at least, they estimated it to be noon. No sun shone to tell—when Camille stopped them abruptly, holding up her hand. "Sh...we draw very close..."

"Close to what?" breathed Aaron.

"I sense a foulness in the air..."

"Probably your breath," Josh muttered, and Krystal, though inwardly gleeful at his comment, glared warningly for him to draw silently.

"I think we are very close...yes, very close indeed..." Her breath quickened, growing shallow. Her chest swelled, eyes gleaming as if in excitement, or perhaps fear. It was hard to tell.

"Draw your blades," she commanded firmly.

"Why? What's going on?" Eric asked as their hands hovered over their swords.

"Just do it—NOW!"

Metal sang as she drew her sword in a lightning-swift flash and the others wielded their blades, and the next moment, innumerable Shadowfolk streamed from the gnarled nests of the branch-like fingers above, from the shadows of their close-knit trunks, from ground, from air, swarming around them like a hive of raging bees, throwing them into the depths of a mad battle.

Fire and lightning raged. Aaron slipped into invisibility, swinging his sword, circling through the air, wielding crazy blows while easily dodging them. Sarah shape-shifted into a wolf, snarling and coming at the enemy with claw and jaw. Rachel, while swinging her sword, tried to turn into an eagle but only managed to get an arm transformed into half a wing, making it overly challenging to swing her sword til she remembered how to change the wing back.

Nathan quickly lost his sword and shimmied up a tree, proceeding to materialize frozen drumsticks and launch them at the Shadowfolk. This seemed to do nothing besides agitate them even further, and they soon aimed arrows up at Nathan who used a tree limb to fend them off.

These Shadowfolk were suddenly knocked off their feet by a giant tree limb soaring through the air.

This came from Chasmira as she wielded her levitation skills. One of the Shadowfolk turned on her, glaring at her with a heartless stare before launching a hatchet at her. His eyes widened as the hatchet catapulted right back at him, pinning him by his cape to a tree, sharp blade narrowly missing his head.

Her eyes flashed dangerously.

"Go, Chasmira!" Rachel shouted, unable to successfully shape-shift into anything besides a fly, resorting to transforming back into her human form and using her sword, landing many violent blows against the enemy.

Hailey meanwhile shrunk the Shadowfolk, scooping as many into one of the empty bean jars as she could, while Sarah hacked with her sword. After changing into a wolf, she took to biting people for a while, but the unfamiliar sensation of sinking her teeth deep into human flesh really wasn't a very pleasant experience, so she turned to her sword skills. She was suddenly thrown to the ground by the blast of a spell from one of the Shadowfolk. Shaking her head to clear the dizziness, she groped at her chest, suddenly realizing...

"My medallion." Her eyes widened in horror.

She shot up, sprinting over to Chasmira. "Chasmira, I've lost my medallion. Have you seen it?"

"No." She fended off a blow with the sword she levitated. Another sword she held in her hands, dodging blows that way simultaneously.

Sarah would've asked the others but knew further distractions could endanger them. So while fending off attacks, she searched the ground for any sign of her medallion.

But then

Suddenly though, she was knocked to the ground as a dull pain pounded on her back, her sword flying from her hands in a wide arc. For a moment, she sat stunned then turned and looked up in stark horror. One of the Shadowfolk held a sword gleaming high above him. She backed away but soon found herself trapped against a tree.

As his sword glowed black, a terrible knowing gripped her. He was going to strike her with the same, unstoppable curse that sent Mr. and Mrs. Daniels to the brink of death. She closed her eyes, took a deep breath, offered a last prayer, braced herself—

"Sarah, catch!"

She opened her eyes to see a medallion spinning through the air like a Frisbee towards her. She caught it, donned it, then glimpsed over to see Chasmira casting a meaningful glance and nod which Sarah returned. The Shadowmen struck at her, the sword piercing her flesh. She could feel its pressure, yet no pain permeated. He pulled the sword out, staring at her, at the bloodless blade, in shocked disgust. She took the opportunity to spring to her feet, grab her sword, and spear him in the side.

Aaron and Eric were meanwhile caught up in a mad furry of sword swinging, turning invisible, then visible, and back again, confusing the Shadowfolk. Josh and Krystal continued their surges of fire and lightning attacks, working as a team, while Sam joined Hailey in her shrinking technique.

The battle raged on all sides. The Shadowfolk seemed to constantly multiply. No matter how many they killed, more seemed to appear until at last their numbers slowly started to dwindle.

"Keep it up!" Aaron shouted in an encouraging tone. "We're beating them back —"

He froze as a terrified scream ripped the air and his heart lurched. He turned to see Chasmira surrounded by the Shadowfolk on every side. She was swordless, her medallion with Sarah, the Shadowmen closed in, there was nothing Aaron could do —

Suddenly, he spotted Camille and called to her, "Camille! Give me your medallion a sec.! And your sword!"

The Dove

Camille stared at him blankly a moment. Then a dark glint illuminated her eyes, a triumphant glint, and she smiled a darkly triumphant smile as she held up her medallion and it transformed into nothing but a plain, ordinary rock.

Instantly, the horrible truth dawned on Aaron. Chasmira had been right about Camille. She led them into a trap. She was a shape-shifter—she changed a common stone to look like the medallion. How did he not see past such trickery..?

Aaron launched himself in Camille's direction then came to a quick halt as she suddenly vanished, no where in sight.

Aaron turned back to Chasmira who cowered on the ground, staring up with wide, fearful eyes. The Shadowfolk closed in on her, one of them raising his blade high. It glowed with an evil black glint. He brought it down—

"NO!"

Suddenly, a bright light intervened. The black blade did not harm Chasmira, rather it seemed to be blocked by a disc of white light hovering between the Shadowman and Chasmira. As Chasmira stared up in wonder and Aaron watched on in awe, they saw the dove, its wings spread wide, glowing with a brilliant, white light. For a moment, Chasmira lay awe-struck, but then she tore past the Shadowfolk who stood dumbfounded though horrified. She dove for her sword and at the same time picked up something else—Sarah's medallion! She donned it and threw herself back into the battle while the dove darted around the Shadowfolk's heads, lacerating their arms, eyes, heads, anything she could sink her claws into.

Finally, after many Shadowfolk lay strewn at their feet, a horn blasted, and the Shadowfolk retreated back into the woods, and, in a flash, vanished.

As they all cheered and congratulated each other on their valiant fighting, Rachel asked, "Wait. What happened to Camille?"

Aaron explained what he witnessed.

"Well, that bum!" Sarah exclaimed. "I knew she was trouble..."

"I think we all did," said Aaron, and all eyes turned upon him. "Except me..."

His tortured eyes could have almost burned a hole of shame into the ground. "I owe you all a major apology, an impossible apology. I put you all in danger, you could've all been killed. When Labrier left me in charge, she advised me to heed the council of my friends. This I have not done. I've been proud and selfish, and I've wasted valuable time on our quest. I should've listened to you all.

"And I owe you an apology especially, Chasmira." He didn't dare look up into those eyes which he knew were so compassionate, understanding, forgiving. Those luminously pleading sapphires would only make him feel all the more unbearably guilty, so he did not look up, at least not until she took his hand. "It's alright, Aaron. I forgive you."

"We all do, man." Josh placed a hand on his shoulder. Everyone concurred.

"We are all of us human, and none of us perfect," added Eric.

Aaron took in a deep breath and smiled sheepishly. "Thanks, guys...thanks for understanding."

"What's important now is that we make up for lost time," said Chasmira. "Do you think we should follow the dove now?"

"There's definitely something about it," mused Hailey. "I mean, Labrier said that the only protection against the Shadowfolk's magic was the medallions, but surely the dove must have some good power within her, right?"

"Well, technically, the dove could've been protected during the fight because it's on their side—"

They all cast Aaron sharp glares, and he added quickly, "But I highly doubt it. So, umm, are we all agreed? Do we follow the dove?"

"We all think it's a good idea, but...you're still the leader." Eric smiled reassuringly, placing a hand on his shoulder. "We go wherever you lead."

[put on his back.]

"Are you sure you guys still trust me?"

"Look," snorted Sarah. "I don't believe I'm about to say this, but...even *I* trust you."

Aaron laughed lightly. The determined sparkle leapt into his eyes once more—Chasmira smiled—and he said, "Well then, let's follow that dove!"

CHAPTER 21

All day they traveled, following the shadow of the dove as she led them. Finally, as the day drew to a close and after trekking deep into the woods, the dove perched upon one of the lofty branches of the trees and sat gazing down expectantly with bright, intelligent eyes.

"Is this it, Dove?" Aaron asked the creature.

The dove cooed and bobbed its head.

"Where's the portal?" Krystal frowned.

"It probably only appears at a certain time, like midnight or dawn or something." Eric shrugged. "You know how these things work...same in real life as in video games, unfortunately..."

As they looked up at the dove in hope of a reply, it only stared down with dark, sparkling eyes.

"Eric could be on to something, and it's all we've got," Aaron agreed. "We'll camp here and set a watch at each hour. I'll go first."

They all settled down for a supper of beans and potatoes(Rachel kept mumbling how much better the meal would be with bacon, and couldn't they at least have stolen Camille's food supplies before she ran off?) then made themselves as comfortable as possible beneath the trees, settling down for a much-needed sleep.

As Aaron sat staring into the black, starlit sky, he found his mind wandering to what lay beyond the portal. What would they find within, on the other side? What new dangers must they face? Yet he was getting ahead of himself in worrying. For now, the major question at hand was the matter of where the portal loomed. They were close, he could sense it. Indeed, as he glanced up at the dove, it stared down with those calm, serene, reassuring eyes. Yes, they were close, but how were they to open the portal?

"Please, Lord," he prayed beneath his breath. "I know I've been a terrible leader, but now I have to make things right. I need Your guidance. *We* need Your guidance, please show us the way..."

* * *

"Man, this whomps," Josh huffed in an agitated tone.

"Jiminy cricket, that's the third time you've said that in the past ten minutes," Rachel muttered, scowling at him. She would've kicked him in her irritation but felt too hot and tired to thus expend her energy.

In fact, they were all hot and agitated. Noon of the next day stretched long, proving to be a windless, scorching afternoon, and still no sign as to what they were supposed to do about the portal showed itself. The dove only sat upon her perch, gazing down at them with that calm, sure, yet anticipating gleam in her eye. This was the spot, or—they hated to for the thought to creep into their heads but it was beginning to—the dove led them astray.

"But it's too coincidental," argued Chasmira as Aaron voiced this possibility, "I mean, Camille not wanting us to follow it, the dove following us everywhere, saving my life—it *has* to be on our side."

"But we can't just sit around and wait for the portal to open."

"Yeah," agreed Josh, "like, it could be a really rare portal that only opens when there's a full moon, or every twenty years, or when a comet falls from the sky, or—"

"Hushy-wa!" Hailey hissed, giving him a very nasty glare. She sat immersed in the process of examining an unusual herb that appeared to open only in the absence of loud noises, and she scowled at him now as the neon, purple petals curled inward sheepishly.

"Aaron's right though," Eric said. "If we stay here much longer, we'll be out of supplies. We really can't afford to stay here longer than a day or so. We'll have to find the portal by tonight or..."

His voice trailed. Everyone glanced at one another, eyes flashing solemn tones. No portal meant no cure for Amanda Danielle and Toby, which meant...

"We'll find it." Chasmira placed an encouraging hand on his shoulder. "Amiel-willing, we'll find it..."

CHAPTER 22

Sarah sat gazing into the remaining embers of the fire. Midnight long ago passed, and with it, the end of her watch. Yet she could not bring herself to awaken Chasmira to take her place. She was so exhausted, urgently needing sleep. Also, Sarah could not find sleep herself, could not rest until she found the answer. She prayed fervently—they all prayed together before going to bed—trying desperately to come up with an answer.

She glanced up at the dove. How could she sit blinking so calmly as though she already showed them the way?

"I need a clue!" Sarah hissed up at the bird. "Can't you give me a clue?"

The dove stared thoughtfully at her for a few moments as if considering the matter, then flew from its perch to sit beside Sarah, tugging at the chain on which the medallion hung.

"What? What is it?"

The dove pulled at the chain for a few moments then let it lie still, sitting frozen as a statue, gazing up with bright, inquisitive eyes.

Sarah cupped the medallion in her hands, running her fingers over the dove etched upon its golden surface which gleamed even within the dark of the night.

"Is the pendant some sort of key to opening the portal?"

The dove cooed softly and bobbed her head once.

Sarah bit her lip, trying hard to remember all Labrier told them about the medallions. They were the only thing that could protect them against the Shadowfolks' attacks, holding the key to repulsing their dark magic...

Suddenly, an insane yet curious idea crept into Sarah's mind. She slowly lifted the pendant over her head, hesitated, then dropped it on the ground—

In a cataclysm of white beams of light, the swirling portal leapt to life before her. How dark its spiraling black and purple shades appeared as the light quickly faded. Evil seemed to radiate from within, carrying on its wings a sharp, cold air that soon woke the others.

"What in tar nation!?" Josh exclaimed, bolting upright.

Sam yawned and mumbled groggily, "I was having such a lovely dream about herbs that shrunk people's noses..."

They would've asked what purpose such an herb would serve, save everyone's attention quickly drew to the portal.

"How on earth..?" breathed Nathan.

"It's the medallions." Sarah used the edge of her tunic to pick hers up. "As soon as they no longer contact your skin, you're left unprotected. Labrier said that they repulse the Shadowfolks' evil magic. Well, that's true. Their protective power has been repulsing the presence of the barrier, but as soon as I took mine off, there was nothing to stand between me and the evil of the barrier..."

Eric nodded. "Good call. And clever of Rorrim. He probably figured we'd never take them off to endanger ourselves."

"About time he did something clever," mumbled Rachel. "Though it *is* a bit late, considering that he's *dead*..."

"Wait." Chasmira frowned. "Does that mean we all have to go through there... without our medallions?"

Apprehensive glances darted between them.

Aaron studied the portal critically. "I guess so...if it's the only way. Though just because we can't wear them to get in doesn't mean we can't sneak them in our knapsacks and put them on once we're inside, does it? I mean, if the only stipulation is they can't touch our skin..."

Murmurs of agreement swept among them, and Eric nodded. "I think Aaron's right. Besides, even if we can't take them in at all, that can't stop us. We can't abandon Amanda Danielle and Toby."

"That's right," confirmed Aaron.

"So, who's going first?" asked Chasmira.

Sarah stepped forth. "I will."

"No," Aaron shook his head. "I'm the leader, I'll lead the way. First, let's all put our medallions away..."

They each carefully slid their medallions into their knapsacks.

Aaron faced the portal, taking in a deep breath. As he plunged inside, he felt someone grab his hand.

Passing through the portal, darkness shrouded him at first, and then, slowly, a grayish light appeared and suddenly he felt firm ground beneath him. He made it. And so did Chasmira.

"Cassy! What're you doing here?"

"I was afraid what might happen if only one of us could get in. I wasn't about to risk losing you again."

He did not scold her, nor would he have been able to. They barely possessed time to share a meaningful gaze and grateful smile before all the others appeared around them.

"Woah, what a rush!" Josh exclaimed. "We totally gotta step into evil portals more often…"

While Sarah gave him a look that read, "You moron," Hailey commented, "Not a very colorful place, is it?"

Grey hills covered with grey, still grass encompassed them on all sides. The sky too stretched like a grey, empty canvas, and even the white-grey sun shone coldly.

Chasmira's eyes suddenly panicked. "Hey, where's the dove? Did we leave her behind?"

Upon hearing a gentle cooing, they looked up. The dove circled overhead then gracefully swooped down and landed. The next instant, there stood before them not a dove, but a young, beautiful, Prismatic woman.

They all stared as Josh breathed his infamous line, "Woah, who's she?"

But before Krystal could think to slap him, they were plunged into an even deeper shock as she replied, "I am Isabel, sister of Tobias."

CHAPTER 23

For a few moments, they could only ogle, uncertain whether to gaze upon her with mere shock, wonder, or horror as if viewing a ghost.

Nathan's face scrunched in painful thought. "But you died. Tobias told us you died…"

Isabel shook her head.

"When Rorrim first ruled Prismatic, during the time Toby was thought to be dead and Amanda Danielle went into hiding in the Garden of Endless Lights, he created a portal to the Shadow World from whence the Shadowfolk come. It is there we now stand. He created a fortress where he could rally the Shadowfolk, meet with them, make plans with them. It is here also he kept all of his prisoners, including me.

"We were all told that if we ever left the Shadow World, if we ever crossed over the barrier, that we would die instantly. Yet by much sneaking and spying, I learned three exceptions existed. Wearing one of the Shadowfolk's medallions such as Rorrim sealed his spirit in, using a warping stone, or shape-shifting into an animal. I knew I could not get my hands on one of the medallions, nor a warping stone, for they were carefully guarded, so I took advantage of the other weakness of the portal, changed into a dove, and passed through the portal back into Prismatic. I have traveled as a dove for many years now, waiting for someone to come and destroy Rorrim once and for all."

"So...Rorrim, if he has no physical body, how can we destroy him?" asked Krystal.

"When the sea serpent attacked you—that was Rorrim."

Wonder spread even more deeply within their faces as they tried to grasp yet another level of the impossible, incredible horrors she told them.

"Yes, Rorrim knew you approached the Prismatic Isle, he knew you held the medallions and would surely try to overthrow him, and, indeed, if Labrier had not intervened..."

"Wait." Chasmira frowned. "Wouldn't the medallions have protected us from the serpent?"

Isabel shook her head. "Against his shadow magic and that of the Shadowfolk, yes. But Rorrim used a different kind of dark magic as the serpent, one that cannot be warded off by the medallions..."

"So..." Aaron's voice quickly trailed as his head reeled, trying to find one point to focus on. "Rorrim was...the sea serpent?"

Again, Isabel shook her head. "Not exactly. You see, when Rorrim sought immortality, he chose to seal his spirit inside a medallion of his own, one bearing his symbol of the black snake. Actually, it is the symbol of the Shadowfolk which he adopted for his own people. The sea serpent itself was originally the Shadowfolks' monster which they gave him to govern and control. The black medallion hangs about the serpent's neck, and through it, he can control the serpent and give it magnificent yet evil powers."

"So to destroy Rorrim," Rachel said slowly, "we must first destroy...the serpent and the pendant?" his spirit rests inside

"Yes." Isabel nodded gravely.

"Then let's get going!" Josh exclaimed, the familiar fire blazing in his eyes. "Where is the beast hiding?"

"In his fortress." Isabel pointed North. "Over these hills."

"Then let's go North," Aaron said.

Isabel nodded then started up one of the long hills, the others following. When they reached the top, both admiration and ominous hatred and disgust filled them. Never did such a massive construction scroll before them, nor such a dark, foreboding, dismal-looking one. The fortress was square-shaped, a looming tower at each of its four corners. There seemed to be no doors in its walls, but they could make out a door in each of the towers facing them. A thick, grey cloud hung over the whole construction.

"Rorrim's Fortress," Isabel hissed, looking upon the fortress as one who returns to prison or some other hated place after years of freedom. Twas not a look of fear but of deep contempt. "Walls run all about the perimeter of the huge courtyard that lies within the center. Tis in the courtyard the serpent makes his dwelling. Come. We have no time to lose..."

Isabel glided solemnly towards the fortress. As they neared it, its massive towers and walls cast gloomy, icy shadows over them, as if both daring and warning them not to come any closer. An evil presence clung to the fortress, a shuddering cold that grew stronger and stronger as they drew closer and closer.

Finally, they stood before the door of the leftmost tower and Isabel explained, "The only way into the fortress is through the towers, and there is only one door leading into the courtyard, but I have not been here in so long that I forget which tower that is. Yet once we enter the fortress, it will lock us inside, so if this is not the tower, we must search for it inside until we come to it. Yet I caution you to have your swords and magic ready. Shadowfolk certainly lurk within."

She cast them each a quick glance to assure they understood the gravity of her words. After they returned her glance with solemn looks, she opened the door and they all filed through.

Immediately, the door slammed shut behind them, the echo of the boom resounding eerily, and a lock clicked. How loud such noises seemed in such ghostly quiet and darkness. For it was very dark. A torch burned further up the tower's wall, casting dark shadows all about them. A door lay to their left.

"No, this is not it," Isabel whispered. "We must go on. Come."

They all moved their hands over the hilts of their swords before walking through the second door.

They passed through a narrow corridor, gliding through the wall of the fortress which suddenly widened and they entered a long room. At first, they stopped in surprise, some taking in their breath. Then they removed their hands from hovering over their swords. Weapons certainly wouldn't be needed here. On either side cold iron bars stretched from floor to ceiling, and behind the bars clustered loads of Prismatics.

The prisoners looked up and gaped at them, and the ten heroes stared in return, as well as Isabel who ogled not only with shock but with a strong, painful sorrow as well.

Suddenly, someone shouted, "It's Isabel! She's come back!"

The prisoners exchanged murmurs then cheers and exclamations.

"Yes!" she cried. "I told you I would come back, my people. It has taken ten years, but I have returned and have brought help with me!"

The people again cheered. Lights of hope illuminated their weary eyes, and the others watched on with hearts pulsing rapidly, eyes brimming. How frail many of them looked, dirt caked onto their clothes, hair, skin. Many bore scars, surely from wounds suffered by the Shadowfolk.

"Isabel!" one voice suddenly called out with frantic passion, and Isabel took in her breath, anxiously scanning the crowd.

"Isabel!" the voice repeated excitedly, on the brink of euphoria.

Then her eyes fell upon him, flooding with tears as she took in a deep, quivering breath. She rushed to him, knelt down, and reached her fingers through the bars. Their hands touched, as did their eyes.

"I didn't recognize you at first." He smiled, lips trembling as tears caressed his face, mingling with the dirt smudged on weary creases. "You look so much healthier, so much better, even prettier. I think being a bird has done you good…"

Isabel laughed lightly though yet crying. "I did not recognize you either. You look terrible."

"Do not cry." He brushed a tear from her cheek. "It will all be over soon, won't it?"

He sought to comfort her, yet she saw the pleading, unsure hope gleaming in his eyes.

"Yes, my love," she answered gently. "It will be. But I must ask: do you know where the entrance to the courtyard lies?"

"Yes."

Isabel rose and turned, ordering, "Please, if I could have your silence for a moment. The heroes and I must hear what Ferdinand has to say."

A reverend hush fell across the room, all eyes focusing upon Isabel and Ferdinand.

"You will find the entrance to the courtyard not in the next tower but the one after. Yet I warn you, the next hallway is said to be guarded day and night by Shadowfolk."

"Why do they guard the next corridor and not this one?" asked Aaron.

"It is said somewhere within that corridor lies the entrance to the room in which are held the black medallions of the Shadowfolk. Therefore, prepare and arm yourselves as you go forth.

"And also I must thank you all. You're the blessing we've all been praying for a long time now."

A series of agreement and thanks rose up from the crowd. The heroes stood smiling humbly yet reassuringly, nodding at the prisoners.

"Please, please..." A voice suddenly called out.

Murmurs rippled as the prisoners receded like an ebbing wave. A small figure, hardly four feet in height, ambled up to the bars. Clad entirely in black, he appeared as a smaller version of the Shadowmen. He gripped the iron bars, tilting his head up though they could not see his face beneath the hood.

"Please, Lady Isabel. I am Warlo, prince of the Shadowfolk. Please, I come to plead on behalf of my people. We did not know of Rorrim's evil. He deceived us into his service, threatened death of our women and children if we did not serve him. Many are beyond hope, minds ensnared by wicked charms. But a few, like myself, still possess our own minds and free will. Please, my lady, please free my people. For many, I know that means death. Yet the sooner Rorrim falls, those few free may be spared...please..."

He slouched down, sobbing, and several women placed comforting arms about him.

"Yes, my sweet Warlo, I will help your people. I do not forget your kindness to me..." She placed a tender hand on his head.

"Thank you, my lady."

Then Isabel knelt once more before Ferdinand and whispered sweetly, "Do not worry, my love. Soon we shall be reunited forever."

He took her hand through the bars and kissed it as tenderly as if handling the purest gold. "I will not worry, and do not worry for me either. I will be praying for you, my sweet heart."

Isabel beamed at him then rose, casting the ten heroes a look that announced it was time to move on.

They bid good-bye to the prisoners, touching the hands stretching out to them as they passed. As their fingertips touched the prisoners' flesh, the contact seemed to ignite their skin with a new warmth, their eyes glowing with a new gleam. The prisoners all the while thanked them, many crying, all promising to pray for their new-found heroes. Rachel even passed several slices of bacon from her secret hoard through the bars to a mother who held a sickly child. Her heart went out to them as the mother thanked her, eyes shining with tears, and the others too gave up much of their food. Besides, their mission catapulted towards a swift end. They now needed only enough for the journey home.

CHAPTER 24

"Hands on your swords," Isabel whispered.

They all did as she commanded, moving their hands to rest over their hilts. They passed through the door into the second tower.

Again, nothing. Only a wide stretch of corridor made of dark, stone walls. It seemed almost too good to be true, and indeed, somehow, they felt it was. Isabel gave them all a look of warning caution before they advanced.

They tread noiselessly down the corridor. All was silence, blackness, and, as they tread deeper into the corridor, soft footsteps echoing loudly, a further and further immersion into a heartless iciness.

As they reached the middle of the corridor, a black arrow zoomed through the air, narrowly missing Isabel's head.

"Attack!" she cried, and instantly they were thrown into battle as Shadowfolk appeared from all sides, seeping like shadows themselves through the walls and surrounding them.

A vicious battle ensued. The heroes could not be harmed because of their medallions, except Isabel who did not wear one, but attacking the Shadowfolk while protecting Isabel proved taxing work.

Suddenly, a great boom resounded, and they all looked over to see Krystal, eyes flashing red and yellow like dancing flames, and a wall of fire suddenly appearing between her and the Shadowfolk, blocking many from reaching the others.

"Alright! I'll hold these guys off and you take care of the rest!"

They briefly thanked Krystal with several shouts and lunged back into battle. Many Shadowfolk still ensued but not nearly as many as before, most blocked by walls of flame, making the battle easier.

Suddenly though, a gut-wrenching shriek jerked their stomachs. Isabel lost her sword and one of the Shadowmen poised over her, prepared to deal a deadly blow—

"Here!" shouted Krystal, lessoning the flames just long enough to take off her medallion and cast it to Isabel. In that brief moment, one of the Shadowmen's swords speared Krystal through the fire. She stumbled but did not fall nor call for help. The wound didn't feel deep, certainly not fatal, but she soon grew weak, forcing herself to concentrate fully on upholding the wall of fire.

As Josh looked over at Krystal, he noticed the pool of blood forming beneath her, the streams of crimson staining her clothes, and stared in horror. He noticed too as she shook her head, trying to free her mind from its cloudy haze, and he rushed over to catch her in his arms as she stumbled back.

"I'll hold them off!" shouted Sarah, forming her own wall of fire against the Shadowfolk.

"Sarah, you can't!" cried Krystal. "You barely started fire lessons before we left for the senior trip!"

"Then let's just say I'm a fast learner. Now, go!"

"Come on," Isabel urged, slaying the last of the Shadowmen on their side of the fire. "Let's hurry."

Chasmira cast a final concerned glance at Sarah who nodded with a reassuring glimmer in her eye.

Together they hurried down the long corridor, Josh carrying Krystal in his arms, worry and reluctant tears undulating within his eyes.

"Josh?" she said softly, gazing up at him. "Are you okay?"

He looked down and saw her eyes searching his. "I'm just worried, that's all. I've nearly lost my sister already. If I lose her, and you too…"

"You're not losing anyone," Krystal said firmly. "Everything will work out."

He smiled faintly at her.

"Stop." Isabel suddenly halted.

They all froze. They found themselves at the foot of another of the towers, and before them hung another wooden door on which a burned, blackened serpent coiled.

"Josh," Isabel's eyes flashed sharply, "Someone needs to stay here and guard Krystal. Can you do that?"

"Of course—"

"No!" Krystal cried. "He needs to be out there fighting. You need him. I won't keep him from fighting just to sit here and—"

Isabel cast her a look that told her no time remained for noble argument and Krystal fell silent.

"If those Shadowmen find you, you will be doomed. You're too weak to defend yourself or the medallion. Josh will stay here and protect you."

Krystal nodded, and Isabel turned to the others. "Come, follow me."

The eight of them slipped through the door.

Again, the single torch burned, casting unfriendly shadows about the tower. Only this time another door loomed across from that they just entered. It too bore the ominous, black serpent.

"Now," said Isabel in a low voice, "We are about to enter the courtyard, which is just to say we prepare to enter the battlefield. The serpent of Rorrim may or may not lurk within. I know not when he comes and goes. Yet if he is not there, I assure you it is only a matter of time. Are you all ready?"

Of course, they all were and they all weren't, eager to defeat Rorrim once and for all though perhaps not so eager to fight a giant serpent. Yet what could they say besides, "Yes?" No coherent choice remained at this point. No other noble decision had ever existed.

They all nodded solemnly and Aaron spoke for them all: "Yes, we're ready."

"Then let us pray together, for guidance, strength, safety, victory…"

Together they held hands and prayed both for themselves, for Sarah, for Josh and Krystal, for the prisoners, and for Amanda Danielle and Toby to hold on just a little longer. Then Isabel grabbed the cold, iron ring serving as both the door's handle and a black serpent's curved fangs, pulled the door open, and together they glided onto the courtyard.

CHAPTER 25

A briefly heartening scrape of metal on metal sang as they drew swords at once, bracing themselves. Nothing surrounded them. Nothing but a wide open expanse of grass and a deep pool in the midst of the fresh green. The green itself seemed too vibrant, its new life out of place, almost tainted in the staunch grey.

Slowly, they ventured forward, gazing at the encompassing, looming walls and towers, closing in and overshadowing them as if mocking, challenging. This was it. No escape remained, they could not turn back.

They dispersed at Isabel's command, wandering in groups of twos to different ends of the courtyard. Perhaps they could surround and confuse the beast and make the battle a bit easier.

Rachel suddenly noticed a slight splash in the water and felt curiously drawn to it, wandering from Tiff's side, eyes locked upon the pool as if entranced.

She approached the edge of the pool and gazed within. The waters were either very deep or very dirty, for they gleamed a deep midnight blue. She could clearly see her reflection, but nothing beyond into the confines of the pool, not even a few inches. It was as though she viewed herself in a black mirror.

Wondering if the water really was dirty or not, Rachel slowly bent over, reaching down the tip of her finger…

"Rachel, no!"

No sooner did Isabel shout, running frantically towards the pool than Rachel's finger tip touched the water and a massive creature shot up, cold, glimmering, sapphire spheres spraying everywhere. The beast waved its head about, letting fly a terrible screech. The serpent loomed, its terrifying fangs and blue scales glistening with a terrible beauty, the black medallion bearing the serpent's symbol dangling from its neck.

It cast a menacing glare and they could almost imagine a cruel smile tugging at its mouth, a smile not unlike Rorrim used to show when a triumphant malice swelled up inside him. They returned the dragon's glare, but this frozen stance of hatred towards the creature lasted only for a moment as immediately he arced down, clashing with his claws, snapping ivory fangs, swishing his mighty tail.

It proved hard enough work just to dodge the creature, let alone landing any hits. They finally developed a strategy, some distracting the dragon while slashing with their swords in hopes of hitting him by chance, others encircling him, trying to shoot arrows. Yet all seemed in vain. None of them were hurt, but the dragon, though he seemed to grow tired, was not affected in the least by their attacks. The arrows bounced off his bright blue scales, the swords drew no blood. Some trick to defeating him must exist, some weak spot, yet what was it?

They had no time to think on the matter though for Shadowfolk suddenly poured in on all sides, over the walls, through the windows and doors, countless numbers gliding noiselessly and stealthily, surrounding them and swathing the serpent to protect it and allow it to recover strength. No longer could the heroes reach the serpent, and now a new battle ensued, the fight against the Shadowfolk.

Warring against the Shadowfolk proved fiercely intense. Though the Shadowfolk could not harm the young adults, they were great in number and skill, keeping them constantly on their toes, forcing the heroes to concentrate on fighting them instead of the dragon.

Rachel performed splendidly with her sword. She suddenly disarmed her tenth Shadowman and prepared to spear him when suddenly she vanished into thin air. The Shadowman looked around, perplexed. Did she turn invisible? Did she warp elsewhere?

Suddenly though, he heard a high-pitched squeaking and looked down. The tiny Rachel who stood no taller than an inch looked livid, her face a bright red. She was yelling something at the top of her lungs, something that he could not decipher except for the mention of the name "Hailey Bodiford."

He had no clue what this meant, but he didn't care. Recovering from his shock, he proceeded to try and stomp on her. He did not stop to think that though she was smaller, she still wore her medallion, and he soon grew frustrated. No matter how much he stepped on her, she didn't ever squish. Rachel too grew very frustrated as the bottom of the Shadow man's boot was very dirty and did not smell at all comely, plus it is very unpleasant and awkward to be constantly squashed without actually squishing.

As Chasmira swung her sword, a terrible thought struck her mind: Sarah—where was she? Hadn't she been warding off the Shadowfolk with her wall of fire? Did their presence mean her demise?

A dread suddenly gripped her as she saw a flash of yellow through the black mass of Shadowfolk. As the Shadowfolk shifted, she espied it—Sarah's medallion clutched in the grip of one of the Shadowfolk's cruel hands. He stared at her with cold, heartless eyes just visible beneath his hood. Chasmira glared back, rushing towards the Shadowman with a cry, hot tears gleaming in her eyes. Hurt and rage flared in her eyes as they beheld the medallion. As Chasmira cried out, the heroes all glanced in her direction to see what was going on, and they too saw the medallion and understood—they had lost one of their own. A new strength and determination for victory surged through them and they launched themselves back into the battle with a new fierceness and resolution to conquer this evil…

Chasmira entered into a fierce struggle against the Shadowman. He proved a skilled warrior, easily and swiftly blocking all her blows. Tears of mixed rage and strange compassion mingled in her eyes. This Shadowman…he could be someone's father, husband, by Warlo's words. How sad it came to this. How odd too she could even feel for him, wonder at his story…

Suddenly, he knocked from her hand and it soared in a wide arc. She dove to get it and felt the Shadowman's shadow pouring over her.

She turned. His sword glowed black. But why? Then she noticed, and her heart sank—her medallion lay a few feet away, its cord shattered. He must have snapped it when he knocked the sword from her hand, but now it was all over, she failed, let Sarah down, let Amanda Danielle down...

Suddenly though, the Shadowman grew stiff as if hit with something, then collapsed to the ground, dead at her feet. Chasmira gasped in horror as she saw the flaming arrow protruding from his bleeding back. Then a shower of the blazing arrows cascaded all around them, hitting only the Shadowfolk. Chasmira looked up and again gasped, staring.

All along the top of western wall stood hundreds of the prisoners, Sarah in their midst, raising her head triumphantly, eyes flashing furiously, her golden-red hair waving like the same flaming embers exhibiting her power, shrouding her with a majestic aura. She reminded Chasmira of Chryselda Sofia, Sarah's favorite, ancient Lozolian princess.

The prisoners stood with bows poised, and as Sarah raised her hand, all arrows were suddenly aglow with fire, and as she raised the other hand clutching her sword, all the prisoners let their arrows rain down upon the Shadowfolk and hundreds fell.

Chasmira caught Sarah's eye for one moment and they smiled at each other, understanding. Their hearts connected with strings of determination, hope, deep friendship, and then—

Sarah bent over in pain, clutching her side, a black arrow protruding from her flesh, and Chasmira remembered she lost her medallion. Sweeping up her own medallion, Chasmira flew up and rushed towards her. Sarah stumbled in pain, plummeting off the wall. One of the prisoners tried to reach out and catch her, but his grasp fell short. Chasmira tried to fly faster but knew she would never make it. Again, the feeling of hopelessness, again those tears returning to her eyes—

At the last moment, Aaron soared forth and caught her, laying her gently on the ground. Finally, Chasmira reached her.

"Stay here with her and protect her," Aaron said. "She's been mortally wounded..."

"Mortally wounded? Blah," huffed Sarah, though in a very weak voice. She forced a smile. "Never mind me. Rejoin the battle."

"No." A tear rolled down Chasmira's cheek. "No, my friend, you have been so brave. You have surely saved us in your valiant efforts. I shall not leave you in your —"

"Oh, cut the poetic stuff. I'm *not* dying," Sarah said firmly, giving Chasmira a defiant look which warned she better not start blubbering about it.

Aaron's lips twitched in a threatening smirk. She probably *was* too stubborn to die. But he only said, "Can you give her your medallion, Cassy? It may help."

"No need." Rachel joined them. "I found hers."

She presented the medallion before rushing off back into the battle, and Chasmira placed it around Sarah's neck.

"May Amiel grant you grace. May He grant you enough time until the dragon is defeated..." whispered Chasmira, stroking the soft silk of her friend's long, silky tresses.

"I must go." Aaron placed a hand on her shoulder, and Chasmira looked up at him. How it pained him as tears glittered in those beautiful green eyes. "Don't worry. We'll all be praying, even as we fight. You <u>know</u> we will."

Chasmira smiled slightly in thanks for these reassuring words, and Aaron soared back into battle.

As Aaron slashed with his sword, he suddenly noticed—the Shadowfolk's numbers dwindled. More arrows rained from the wall, and though they no longer held the power of Sarah's fire, Shadowfolk still fell all around.

A hope struck him. Could he reach the dragon? Through the masses of Shadowfolk he could see the dragon triumphantly surveying the battlefield. So Rorrim still thought he could win, did he? Aaron decided to make a break for it. After all, he knew how to do one thing only few Shadowfolk ever mastered—flight.

He soared up, a bit unsteadily at first, but then confidently surged towards the dragon. A few Shadowfolk leapt in his way, but he quickly dispatched them. For a moment, his eye met the dragon's. He stared into Rorrim's eyes, the familiar contempt gleaming vividly in the dragon's dark spheres, though this time, if possible, the hatred flared greater and deeper than ever.

Aaron rushed up to the dragon but a swipe of his massive tail quickly threw him back against one of the walls. Aaron glared defiantly at the dragon. Maybe Rorrim could not hurt him, but he wasn't going to give him an easy win either.

Aaron flew up, narrowly dodging the creature's tail. He speared his side, but nothing happened. He tried his back leg, his neck, his front leg, all the while dodging the tail's blows. Surely the dragon must possess a weak spot? Wait. The tail. Its scales shone a brighter blue than the rest of the creature's body. Perhaps he must attack the tail to proceed.

But how? He could not get close enough without getting beaten back by the mightily thrusting limb.

Suddenly, the creature roared in pain, clawing at its eye. One of the prisoners stood poised on the wall, bow ready to shoot again, and he did, right into the dragon's other eye.

Aaron took his chance while the enraged dragon was distracted and speared the tail. The blue scales fell away completely from the dragon's tail, leaving only soft, tender skin in its place. Yet also, his front legs now glowed bright blue, and Aaron, suddenly understanding the gist of the battle, attacked the arms. The scales fell away and his back legs gleamed...

Isabel, Tiff, and Rachel suddenly looked up as blue scales cascaded all about them like falling stars. They watched for an admiring moment as Aaron hacked at the dragon then rushed to help him. Most of the Shadowfolk lay slain about them, and the few remaining were dispatched of by the boys and Hailey.

Soon though, Hailey, Eric, and Nathan could stop their work against the Shadowfolk as all lay dead about them, and they too took to disarming the dragon of its scales. The Dragon flailed blindly, whipping its tail madly, slashing furiosuly with its claws, but all in vain. Soon it stood completely stripped of armor, and everyone, from the prisoners on the walls to the friends fighting down below lacerated the dragon's tender skin with both blade and arrow until finally, with a hideous screech, it crashed to the ground, sending tremors echoing through the earth.

Aaron lifted his blade, facing the creature which opened one of its bloody eyes just the tiniest bit. Whether it could see him or not, Aaron was never sure, but all the same, he returned the serpent's icy stare with one of his own, one of determined triumph. His heart racing, he speared the black medallion. Immediately, cracks raced all along the medallion's surface, glittering with a bright white light. The entire dragon glowed, and Aaron stepped back as a strong wind swirled all about his giant frame. Everyone watched in awe and anticipation as the light faded, and there lay in the dragon's place only a pile of blue and black ashes. The dragon was no more. Rorrim was no more. He was defeated, both body and spirit, at last.

At first, everyone could only stare. But then a voice broke the silence: "Well, what're we waiting for? Let's get the heck out of this crummy place!"

"Sarah!" cried Chasmira, turning back to her. She sat up smiling, her wounds completely healed. They embraced, and soon everyone else rushed over to see how she was doing then congratulate each other on a battle well fought.

Isabel walked up and placed a hand on Aaron's shoulder. "You did very well. You have both proven a good leader and a good friend. Amanda Danielle will be proud."

He smiled at her. Someone suddenly swept her up in a hug though, and turning, she saw that not only Ferdinand, but also all the other prisoners already climbed down from the wall, joining them in the courtyard.

Isabel smiled upon her people, beaming larger still as Ferdinand took her hand and kissed her lightly on the cheek. *including the remaining, rescued Shadowfolk*

"Finally," he breathed. "I finally got my first kiss."

Isabel looked up at him and for a moment they shared a gaze reflecting their *—they were all her people—* deep love for each other. Tears gripped her eyes as the overwhelming realization gripped her heart. Freedom. Freedom at last to love him and be loved by him forever...

But then Isabel remembered the others and turned to the prisoners. "Now, my good people, I shall take you to the Prismatic Palace. Then I shall fetch your queen and king. Surely they have awakened by now and will want to see you all safe and sound. Now, we must all join hands..."

The hundreds of heroes did so, forming a wide circle along the perimeter of the courtyard, a beautiful ring of Prismatics, students, and elegantly cloaked Shadowfolk.

"Now, Chasmira, the stone," said Isabel.

Chasmira stared at her, perplexed. "The stone?"

"In your pocket."

Chasmira reached in pulled out the blue, shimmering, warping stone.

Her eyes lit up with excitement. "I totally forgot I had this."

"Yeash, *now* she remembers. We could've really used that before, you know, like when freaky Shadowfolk were attacking us—owe!"

Krystal gave Josh a hard kick and he returned her nasty glare, muttering, "Yeash, woman, I was just kidding...glad you're feeling better though, love..."

"So you think it will work?" Chasmira looked up at Isabel hopefully.

"It should. Let's give it a try."

Chasmira held out the stone to Isabel who took the stone in her hand. Yet before uttering a word, she cast a final glance around the prison that served as her home for so long, the prison she stood finally freed from. No longer did the grey seem so melancholy, the walls so hopelessly tall. The walls were just walls, the grey just a normal grey. She laughed lightly as the elated realization dawned upon her.

Her eyes fell upon the mound of ashes now piled in the courtyard's midst, gazing pensively for a few moments.

"Rorrim—a pitiful man...In his lust for immortality, he never learned how to live a good life on earth, nor did he ever learn that it is not this life, but the next, that matters most of all..."

She stood there a few moments more, then she looked up, clutching both the stone and Ferdinand's hand tightly, shouting, "To the Prismatic Palace!"

Immediately, they stood inside the great hall. Servants just waking from sleeps of enchantment gazed about awe-struck. One of them, an elderly woman, teetered up to Isabel and breathed, "Isabel, my lady, is that really you?"

"Yes, Elenor. I have returned."

Tears filled her eyes and she clapped her hands. "I always believed you were still alive. I always kept prayin' too." Glancing around at the prisoners, her eyes grew wide.

"Who are all these poor folk, my lady?"

"They are the prisoners of Rorrim's fortress. We have just returned from overthrowing him. They need food and clothing. Can you get the servants to attend to them?"

"Yes, my lady, yes." She curtsied several times excitedly.

"Thank you. I am sure the king and queen shall be grateful for your service as well."

Elenor's eyes grew even wider.

Isabel smiled brightly. "Yes, the king and queen live. They shall return to you shortly."

"Lord be praised!" cried the servant, immediately rallying the servants, cheerfully calling out orders. Chasmira smiled, heart swelling with joyous tears as she watched an elderly woman grasp Warlo's hand, stopping to whisper kind words as she led him along with the other prisoners.

"Now." Isabel turned to Aaron and the others. "We must fetch Amanda Danielle and Toby."

They all took hands, and after casting a final smile in Ferdinand's direction, Isabel took out the stone and shouted, "To the tomb of Amanda Danielle and Toby!"

In a flash, they stood before the tomb. The door loomed wide open. Labrier must be inside.

Bright sunlight poured into the tomb so no torches were needed as they hurried within, hearts racing with excited anticipation.

Yet as the door opened and they stepped inside the room with the stone tables, they stopped, staring in complete disbelief. The tomb was empty but for the tables and the pillars of light. They all glanced at each other worriedly. Where were Amanda Danielle and Toby? Was it too late?

Yet, suddenly [Then], they heard Labrier calling, "Hello? I said, 'you can come out of there!'"

They all cast each other curious, hopeful glances then [and] scurried down the corridor.

Upon reaching the entrance of the tomb, they stopped short, took in their breath, stared up in wonder, awe, admiration...

Amanda Danielle and Toby stood in the doorway, Labrier behind them. The sunlight behind cast glorious rays all about the couple, illuminating their hair and causing it to shine with the same, brilliant, white glimmer as when they first sailed to Prismatic.

Their faces beamed, and Amanda Danielle said in her soft yet strong, clear voice, "Welcome, my children. I thank you all once again for your courage and bravery, and for restoring peace once again to our Isle of Prismatic.

"Isabel..." Taking notice of the Prismatic princess, she took in a sharp breath. Toby stared hard as if trying to determine whether he still slept in the tomb, whether the sight before him was so wonderful that he must yet slumber...

"How can this be..?" He whispered in awe.

"My brother..." Isabel flew into his arms. His own arms closed about her in a very real embrace. Such an overwhelming, indescribable joy could not be dreamt.

Amanda Danielle hugged her too then gazed upon Isabel, eyes glittering both with tears and unmasked rejoicing. "What a glorious day Amiel has given us. He restores to me not only my life, my husband, my children, but my sister as well."

They shared a meaningful smile, tears gleaming within both ladies' eyes. Then Amanda Danielle turned to the others. "Well, I'm already misting. You may as well come and give me a hug too."

After the hugs were exchanged, prayers of thanks offered up, and after a brief account of their adventures in which Isabel told the king and queen their people waited for them at the palace, Toby beamed at them all, never looking more kingly as he declared, "Come. We must return to the palace. There is much to celebrate."

CHAPTER 26

The ten friends stood upon the deck of the ship, leaning over the railing and staring out over the peaceful waters and beautiful sunset. How glorious the feast at the palace was, especially visiting with the prisoners who already looked healthier and so much happier. And finally, parting with Amanda Danielle and Toby, they promised to come visit again. This time, she granted full permission to use the warping stone as often as they pleased, so long as they didn't skip classes. They readily accepted this invitation though the guys didn't necessarily sound sincere about not skipping classes. Of course, they could've used the stone to go back home, but since they were gypped out of quite a bit of their senior trip, Amanda Danielle offered them one of her magic, lily-laden ships to travel home on, assuring their travels would prove calm and peaceful this time. And they needed exactly that, a refreshing, restful trip [respite] before returning to school.

So the morning following the feast, after little Cooper grabbed Josh's nose for the tenth time and after little Mirabel pouted and threw her food at him, they boarded the ship that would carry them home.

Thankfully, they would reach Loz by morning. They were grateful too for the calm voyage home, the proper clothing, and, especially for the girls, showers. Krystal also felt thankful to find inside the ship a shop that sold her favorite lipstick, and to Tiff who lent her money to buy some.

Sam sighed contentedly as he gazed out over the ocean. "Another adventure over and done with. And some new herbs discovered. That makes it the best adventure of all, you know."

"Yes," agreed Hailey. "Herbs...how lovely..."

Rachel shrugged. "Well, it *was* sort of fun, I suppose. Though I didn't much like that Shadow guy stepping all over me."

Everyone laughed. Then a few more minutes of serene, thoughtful silence ensued as they gazed out over the ocean reflecting the sunset's brilliant colors.

"Hey, you know what," Rachel broke the quiet. "There's still one thing we never found out. Sarah never told us how she escaped from all those Shadowfolk."

"Oh, yeah." Sarah laughed to herself. "Ahh, I remember. More and more Shadowfolk started showing up. I was surrounded on all sides and knew I wouldn't be able to hold them off any longer, and I certainly wouldn't do anyone any good if I got captured and locked in a cell or something. Suddenly, one of the idiot Shadow-dudes was grabbing the chain of my medallion and choking me, so I turned myself into a fly but didn't shrink the medallion to accommodate my size. The Shadowman held my medallion, perplexed, and I buzzed off to set the prisoners free and rally them. One of the Shadow prisoners knew where the weapons were, and, well, things just went pretty smoothly from there."

Josh couldn't stop laughing at the thought of Sarah being a fly for some reason, and thus Sarah leaned over to Chasmira and whispered, "Okay, I promised to tolerate Aaron, and he's not so bad anymore, but how do you stand *him*?"

Chasmira laughed lightly, "He's really not so bad either. You'll get used to him."

Sarah only glanced at her doubtfully.

"I still wonder what became of Camille." Krystal leaned further over the railing.

"Well, she *did* fail Rorrim," said Sarah. "Maybe he turned her into a fat toad."

"Or a moose," suggested Hailey.

"Probably turned *herself* into a toad to get away from Rorrim," Rachel snorted. "At least, that's what *I* would've done...Well, maybe not a *fat* toad...or maybe not a toad at all...a horse maybe..."

"*Or*," Josh suddenly drew his dramatic air which caused Krystal to roll her eyes, "She's out there right now, impersonating one of us and wreaking havoc, destroying our reputations..."

"Well, no worries for you." Krystal smirked slyly. "You're already known for wreaking havoc."

"That's true," agreed Josh. "Plus, well, I don't really think anyone could pull off my unique charm and...manliness..."

As he stood tall and puffed out his chest, Krystal poked him in the ribs which sent him giggling and everyone laughing.

"See," whispered Aaron to Rachel. "I *told* you guys could giggle..."

For a while after, they just stared out at the sun setting beneath the horizon, the ocean sparkling in a wondrous array of pinks, oranges, and yellows.

Chasmira sighed and breathed, "Isn't it beautiful?"

"Yes it is," Aaron returned, and she felt her hand slip into his.

They smiled at each other, and as Chasmira gazed deeply into his eyes, she sighed again, contentedly. Aaron was himself again, and they were going home—together. But together in a different way than when the trip started. Together not only physically, but their hearts too began to knit closer. She could feel those threads slowly but surely entwining. A new and different sort of journey began for her, for *them*, and she thanked Amiel silently.

CHAPTER 27

The ten heroes rested most of the day. It felt good to snuggle in their warm canopy beds and sleep peacefully once more. "All that being crammed in a tent with Nathan and Eric gave me cramps," Josh complained.

As supper drew near, the girls headed towards the dining hall when someone called, "Chasmira, can I please talk to you a moment?"

They stopped and turned. It was Eric.

"In private. Perhaps in the garden?"

Chasmira and the other girls glanced at each other curiously before She replied, "Sure, Eric."

She followed him into the garden. An odd expression masked Eric's face. He appeared very pensive yet seemed to be trying to hide the trouble undulating in his eyes. He led her very slowly to a shady tree then faced her.

"Chasmira." His bright blue eyes seriously gripped hers. "I must go away for a while. I do not know when I shall return to Lynn Lectim."

"Where are you going?" Chasmira asked softly, immediately concerned. Eric's gaze drifted from hers. He *was* troubled about something. Incredibly so.

He remained silent a little while, taking several deep breaths, struggling between reply and further silence.

"It is very important, but—" Here his eyes met hers again, flashing yet more seriously—"also very secretive. I cannot tell you where I am going or how long I shall be away. But I *shall* return."

He reached into his pocket, presenting a jade green bracelet.

"It was my sister's. I want you to have it."

"Your sister? I didn't know you had one."

"She...she died when we were young. Julie was her name." Again, his gaze drifted, only this time his eyes gleamed not just with torment but sorrow too.

"Eric, I couldn't possibly—"

"Chasmira, please take it." His gaze rested once more upon her. Taking her small hand in his, he slipped the bracelet onto her delicate wrist. "You are the most wonderful, charming, enchanting person I've ever met. I never cared about anyone so much. You have become my dearest friend in the short time I've known you, Chasmira Eriz, and I want you to have it. I think Julie would've wanted you to have it too. You said once that you wear green every day in Aaron's honor, so I thought you would like it, though I hope you will remember me sometimes when you wear it too."

"I will," Chasmira returned quietly, smiling. "Thank you, Eric."

"I must go now. Good-bye, Chasmira, until we meet again."

"Good-bye, Eric."

Then he turned and slipped through the bushes.

Chasmira stood staring pensively after him for some moments when she found herself fumbling with something in her pocket—the moon blossom Eric gave her. Its petals opened and sparkled brightly as the moonlight touched them. Chasmira suddenly thought that perhaps she could give it to Eric so he would have something to remember her by as well. She hurried through the garden, searching until she saw a light emanating from the phoenix clearing and rushed towards it. She emerged into the clearing just in time to see Eric standing and holding a round, glowing object in his hands, and then, in a flash, he disappeared and everything lay still once more.

Chasmira stood in silence until she heard someone calling her name. It was Aaron, and Nathan and Rachel followed him into the clearing.

"What're you doing out here?" Aaron asked Chasmira.

"Eric wanted to see me before he left."

"He left?" Rachel's eyes bulged. "*Again*? Third time in three years..."

Chasmira nodded. Her gaze remained distant as she wondered what Eric was about, where he vanished so quickly.

Nathan shrugged. "Well, that's Eric for you. Always coming and going."

Aaron took her hand. "Chasmira, are you okay?"

Chasmira finally snapped out of her reverie and turned towards them.

"Yeah." She smiled.

"Come on then. Let's head back before Josh hogs all the chicken again."

He squeezed Chasmira's hand and together they led the way back to school.

* * *

Circling all about, her eyes darted frantically. Where was he? She hadn't seen him in months. She was used to long, painful spans of time slipping slowly, devoid of his presence, but this...this didn't feel right.

Think, think, think...where did he appear in book three? His appearance seemed so isolated. She could picture his face as she shut his eyes tight, but what was he doing, where was he going, what was he feeling..?

She gasped, staring out into the crowds of socializing, unaware teens as if they all faded away or else merged into a great wall of ominous blackness. A single scene, not even showing him but mentioning him as if he were less than the despised, secondary character everyone loathed him as, a scene in which she'd had to contrive much in her imagination—his screaming, pleading, torture-ridden face, wide, begging eyes, contorting, writhing body—

Bursting forward, only half-hearing the cries of those she ran into, she raced, stumbling, pushing, clawing through the bodies, unable to move fast enough, her feet failing her as she catapulted herself from the room, down the hall, towards the men's bathroom—

Springing in, she found no one, heard nothing. *Which bathroom?* she cursed beneath her breath. Perhaps the west wing. It was closest to his room, after all...

Approaching the west wing's bathroom, she slowed her pace, treading with muffled footsteps as a sound drifted towards her ear, the wisps of a pitiful wailing, soft sobs, and a voice muttering incomprehensibly. Sidling towards the door, she peered her head around...

He leaned against one of the sinks, hands clutching the sides tightly, shaking violently all over, wretching the nothing that remained to throw up, then choking on great sobs, whispering eerily, all strength and hope drained from his voice, "It's all falling apart...all of it...slipping away..."

She took a step forward, loudly to make her presence known.

He whirled, and before the scream could half slip from her throat, the wave of power knocked hard into her chest, jerking the breath from her as she crashed to the floor, head throbbing as it hit the cold marble.

"Tiffany?" he gasped in horror, then his face hovered over hers as he knelt. For a moment, it faded in and out fuzzily, yet as her vision cleared, tears caught in her own eyes. His face shone even paler than usual, a sickly white instead of his normal, alluring sheen. Dark circles clung beneath dark eyes illuminated wide with horror at what he'd done and an even deeper terror at what was further expected of him.

"I'm okay," she assured, struggling to hold back the tears, feeling he'd seen enough in the past months. "But where have you been?"

"I can make myself invisible too now, you know," he said, smiling feebly, a ghostly smile that in no way met his eyes. "You should know..."

"The book says so little of you during this time," she whispered. "Please...tell me what's wrong, Dristann, I never thought I would see you this way..."

He began to shake again. The orange-red glow of the bathroom's torches cast an extra-strange glimmer upon his pale, wraith-like features. Fear and pity mingled within her as he breathed, "She's dead, Tiffany, my mother's dead..."

"What?" she gasped. "The Dark Enchantress...so you're no longer..?"

"No," he scoffed. "I know, what's the difference, right? I still don't go out in the sun, skin fair as winter's first snow, annoying, strong powers, obviously..." His eyes flickered with hurt... "but she is dead, and what has the lifting of her gift granted me save to make me more vulnerable. She has asked me already, Tiffany, my aunt...Before my mother died, she quarreled with my mother. Their lust for power finally caught up with them so that they waged against each other. My aunt came to me, threatening that I must help her carry out her plan or she'd kill my mother and I both...I guess it's too late for my mother...

"But she still wants me to do it, Tiffany. She's tired of me screwing up, of my half-hearted attempts at helping her. If she doesn't succeed, she'll make me kill her or else...or else she'll kill me...She already plans in usurping my mother's throne if she succeeds, thinking that I will use my powers to take it from the queen the Stregoni have set up. I don't give a care about that throne, no one in that kingdom hardly knows I exist, I want to be rid of it, as though it never was...

"But...but I must do it, Tiffany," his voice sunk to a tremulous whisper, lips sputtering as his whole body shook with the uncontrollable fear gleaming in his wide, luminous eyes, "there is no choice...if she doesn't die, then my aunt will make certain I do..."

"Dristann, you have a choice, you don't have—"

"There is no choice!" he cried, his voice almost pleading her to make a choice possible, "I don't want to die, I don't want to die alone and leave you. I'm afraid, Tiffany, so afraid...You told me once my story does not end well, I know you can't tell me anything beyond but if you could just help me, please..."

"I would help you, but not in the way you ask," she replied, her voice soft as a zephyr as the tears streamed unrestrained down her cheeks now, his pain too unbearable for her to bear. "I won't help you kill anyone. You are not a murderer, Dristann, to do so would split your fragile soul in two, irreparable pieces. But run away with me, Dristann, to another world where no one can find us—"

"No, she would, she would find me—"

"Listen!" she cried, reaching up to caress his bent, trembling face. "Please...there is a way..." She hesitated, suddenly nervous despite the seriousness of the situation, but his tormented, begging eyes convinced her... "there is a way in which you could be granted the same protection rights as a Story-traveler, even if we returned to this world. You would be safe from dying, from sustaining permanent injury, just like me if...if you married me," she added in a quick whisper, glancing away timidly. She continued, "Of course, you don't have to, I wouldn't make you if you don't love me the same or if you just didn't want to, but it's an option—"

She gasped, looking up at his face hovering so close to hers now as he laid on his side beside her, staring at her as if she were the most wondrous sight in all the world, his eyes imploring, as if searching to ascertain her words were true, her offer sincerely meant, that he was sincerely...wanted...

Her breath quickened, stomach churning as he slipped a hand beneath her head. Her body grew rigid as his eyes closed, as he lowered his lips to hers...

The tension released as his lips hugged hers and as she hugged them back, kissing fervently, their lips gracefully caressing each other's as if always meant to be together. She shuddered as he massaged her neck, his fingers trailing down her shoulder, her arm, her thigh as he hovered over her, pressing his body close against hers as if that kiss fused them into one person, healing the wounds that severed their hearts as those two hearts merged into one entity...

When his lips finally departed softly from hers, he looked at her with newfound wonder, much of the fear dissipated as he smiled, a sincere, hopeful, though yet sorrowful smile.

"Please, Dristann," she pleaded gently. "You don't know how it hurts to see your hurt and know I can help you if only...I know you're scared, but if you'll only trust me, come with me, I promise I'll do all in my power to make sure it was worth it..."

His eyes hesitated so longingly locked on hers, so desiring to trust...

Suddenly, footsteps approached. His eyes glared up as someone rounded the corner into the bathroom.

"What are you doing to her?" the boy snarled.

"Can't you keep your nose in your own business, Ruiz?" Dristann hissed.

Aaron launched a ball of flame which Dristann quickly blocked, springing up as Tiffany shouted, "Stop it, you two!"

She scrambled to sit up, screaming at them to stop, but her cries fell in vain as Aaron released another volley of fire, eyes blazing with many years of pent-up frustration. Dristann's eyes matched his as he thrust all his pain and torture back at Aaron with his attacks.

"Stop it, please!" she continued to plead, following them as they slipped into the depths of the vast bathroom, fire, shadows, various other magics rebounding off the walls, slamming the stall doors wide open, exploding toilet paper which fluttered about like falling snow. A sink suddenly exploded, spraying water everywhere, blinding her, but the moment she forced her way through its spray, she shrieked in horror—

The scene seemed to scroll in slow motion, like some dream too awful to believable, yet one which won't just end the torture, prolonging it. He fell, crashing into the water, thrashing as the fire consumed one side of his body, blood pooling beneath him from unseen wounds while Aaron stood, motionless, eyes wide with the realized dread of the scene happening too slowly yet too real before him as well...

She sprang to his side, voice trembling as she muttered the water spell, the water flowing up over him to extinguish the flames. But flames leapt in her burning heart, searing her eyes as she spat at Aaron, "How *could* you?! You have *no* idea what he's been going through!"

"I—"

"Don't just stand there, get him to the hospital wing, you idiot!"

Jumping, he rushed to carefully heft Dristann in his arms, groaning as he lifted the dead weight, glancing down as Dristann moaned, then away at the sight of mingled burns and blood scathing his body. Leaping up, he hovered a moment then flew through the air as fast as he could, Tiffany racing after him, cursing her feet which couldn't travel fast enough as he zoomed out of sight.

She stumbled as the tears blinded her, but she neither stopped nor slowed, even when she passed people asking if she was alright as she gasped for breath, even as she at last approached the hospital wing, scaled the tower steps, burst into the room...

He already lay sleeping beneath the white sheets, his skin yet glowing red from the heat but the burns and blood dissipated. Aaron slouched wearily on a chair, a ghostly fear echoing in his eyes as he watched Dristann. Pulling up a chair beside him, she whispered, "How's he doing?"

"Nurse says he'll be fine since I got him here so quickly," he mumbled. "I told her we were messing around with spells...I never realized how powerful I could..." His voice trailed and he swallowed hard.

After some time, he said, a wonder in his voice, "You really care about him, don't you?"

"I love him," she corrected ardently, gazing with a deep pain and admiration upon his face, so wearily troubled even in sleep.

"How?" It was not an accusation, not sarcastic, but a calm, sincerely awed question.

"Because I know things...secrets of what he's been through and goes through still...and I see things no one else sees...When we're together, it's like I calm him, I make him able to show his gentler side, his sweetness. All else fades away, I can make him forget everything but us for a time..."

"I am sorry," he breathed.

"I know," she whispered. "I know."

Rising, she walked over to sink gently onto the edge of the bed, caressing his face, shuddering as she felt one blazing hot cheek, then the other, so abnormally cool. He moaned softly, then a smile tugged at the corners of his lips, the furrow in his brow lifting a bit...

She smiled sadly at Aaron. "See..."

"I think it's good...what you're doing for him. I know I don't understand, but...it's good he has someone..."

"You don't have to wait," she said gently.

"No...but I will. To apologize and try to see the worth in him that you do. Maybe we don't have to be friends, but it's time our quarrel ended before we hurt each other permanently..."

Her eyes smiled proudly at him. Then her gaze returned yet more proudly to the face of the man she loved, and laying her head beside his, she slept with him.

* * *

Aaron descended the mansion's stairs, slipping into the confines of the garden, taking great gulps of needed yet unsatisfying air, mind whirring as he replayed the scene an over again in his mind…

Dristann awakening, staring at him with hard but questioning eyes, listening gratefully and accepting his apology, casting a lingering, sleepy smile upon Tiffany as though she was some impossibly brilliant angel before drifting back to sleep. Tiffany thanking him for his apology and saying with an uncanny, uneasily knowing foreboding in her voice, "I am glad you have made peace. For a time approaches when that shall become either a difficulty or an impossibility altogether."

Her eyes gazing deeply into his for a few, hard moments, an intricate message etched within those eyes, a message only she could understand and which he could only decipher, he feared, when the time she spoke of came and all was too late. What warning echoed within her words? How grateful he was when her eyes broke from his to guard over her Dristann as she stroked the white-blonde hair back from his face, now returned fully to its normal, snowy shade, a healthy flush creeping back into his cheeks…

"Aaron?" Chasmira's voice called to him, distantly it seemed at first, until he allowed the cheery strain to rent his brooding thoughts.

She burst through the trees into view, like a single stream of light parting the heavy storm clouds weighing on his heart. He smiled at her as she said breathlessly, eyes sparkling with that innocent, child-like joy, "I hoped I would find you here. You're missing the term's ending feast, the chocolate cake is extra scrumptious. Aren't you coming before Josh hogs it all and transforms it into asparagus?"

He chortled quietly. Then, silently, he took her hand, allowing her to prattle on as she pulled him enthusiastically back towards the mansion. If Tiffany's words meant little time remained, whatever the snatching away of that time signified, then he would wait to worry about the ending of that time when it came. For now, he would spend these residual serene moments as Tiffany did, in the comforting presence of his truest love, his calm before whatever storm lay ahead.

THE END

THE HERO CHRONICLES
BY CHRISTINE E. SCHULZE

THE HERO OF 1000 YEARS

HEROES REUNITED

THE DOVE

THE SECRET SISTER AND THE SILVER KNIGHT

THE PRINCESS OF DESTINY AND THE PRINCESS OF
THE NIGHT

Made in the USA